I0552408

BOOKS BY SUZA KATES

The Savannah Coven Series
Whisper of a Witch
Conviction of a Witch
Binding of a Witch
Haunting of a Witch
Possession of a Witch
Deception of a Witch
Suffering of a Witch
Boys' Night Out (E-novella)
Vengeance of a Witch
Sacrifice of a Witch

The Sisters' Grimoire Trilogy
The Sisters' Grimoire (Novella)
Winter Fae
Chosen Blood

Single Titles
Hallowed Eve
The Penance Stone
She Who is Hidden

CHOSEN BLOOD

THE SISTERS' GRIMOIRE TRILOGY

SUZA KATES

ICASM PRESS
SAVANNAH

Published by Icasm Publishing LLC
5710 Ogeechee Rd. Suite 200 #278, Savannah, GA 31405
www.icasmpress.com

Library of Congress Cataloging-in-Publication Data

Kates, Suza
Chosen Blood / Suza Kates
    p. cm.

ISBN-13:978-1-942318-23-1
ISBN-13:978-1-942318-24-8 (Mass Market)
ISBN-13:978-1-942318-25-5 (ebook)
I. Title

ACKNOWLEDGEMENTS

An author is the beginning of a book, but the final product wouldn't exist without the help of others. My heartfelt thanks goes to Mandi Cranson, Sharyn Cerniglia, and Donna Wood for their continued hard work. Editing isn't just about commas but also involves cheerleading, counseling, and a boatload of patience!

For this particular story, I want give a nod to Adele Pugsley. When I couldn't think of a name for a handsome black horse, she stepped in with the winner! Thank you, Adele, for naming Dante. It was the perfect fit!

To Dorothy Beecher and Stella Racicot, your friendship has been invaluable, and now your help on the books as well. Thank you so much for dipping into the crazy!

Finally, I have to thank my husband, David, and there aren't enough words to tell him how appreciative I am. The last two years have been a trial, and I am so glad to have had such a caring man by my side through all the ups and downs. (Including those dark moments that called for emergency pizza and caramel popcorn)

And to the readers, thank you for continuing to read my stories. Your support and kind comments are the always the best reward.

1

Spindly black legs clicked over the fractured stones as the giant cretid closed in on Fiona. Back pressed against a high stone wall, she tried to keep the predator in sight, but all around her, gray mists slithered, crawling through the Ruins of Morogost like ravenous ghosts.

As if in league with the insect-beast, the fog thickened and swirled, blocking her view. And it was cold. So cold.

She could still hear the legs—*click-click-click*—but all she could see was the creature's curving tail. Glistening with venom, the barb jutted forward. Then the tail lifted higher, poised to strike.

Fiona's heart began to thump, one shuddering beat after the other, shooting a savage throb through her bloodstream. A throb of terror.

The cretid emitted one awful screech and lurched.

Sensing the attack, Fiona flung up her arm, but the monster's jab was swift and true, its sharp tail stabbing deep into her chest. Poison and pain shockwaved into her body, paralyzing her limbs and stealing the very oxygen from her lungs.

Yet even as her system revolted, her mind clamped onto reason. And something worse than poison surged in her veins, a noxious mixture of shame and defeat. How did she get here, to the once-glorious courtyard of a distant world?

She pressed a hand to her lethal wound. How could she have let this happen again?

As if summoned by Fiona's surge of remorse, her sister Tate appeared suddenly beside her. "You failed, Fiona." She shook her head, her lips tight. The disappointment carving Tate's frown cut more deeply than the cretid's tail.

"I'm sorry," Fiona said, trying to remember what she'd done. But all she knew was that she'd made a terrible and costly mistake. "I tried. I—"

Bolts of lightning cracked in the sky, illuminating the mists with an eerie green glow.

Tate cocked her head, as if sensing something other than the storm. Ignoring Fiona, she slowly turned and slipped away.

"Tate!" Fiona cried, but only howling winds answered. One blink, and her sister was gone, swallowed by the growling mists.

Fiona's blood seeped freely from her wound, tinged black by the poison it now carried. She pressed both hands to her chest, but the stain continued to spread. "I can't fix it. I don't know what to do."

Lightning snaked down—louder now, closer—and like before, the strike glowed green. From within the strange light, her other sister emerged. Sami floated over the ground, her gypsy-brown eyes empty, void of life.

"Fee, how could you?" She reached out, her face a mask of despair. "We are all lost, and you will never find us."

"I will, Sami. I'll make things right." Fiona stretched out to take her sister's hand, but something held her in place. She looked down to find herself ankle-deep in bright, shimmering jewels.

Rich and enchanting, the gems promised like prayers. They gleamed like wishes.

But their beauty was a lie.

When she looked again, Sami was gone.

"Tate! Sami!" She called for her sisters, taken by the fog. She summoned her magick, but none rose to her aid.

Abandoned, drowning, she slipped deeper and deeper.

And this time when lightning hit, deep male laughter rolled

beneath the thunder.

Fear fisted in her gut, and Fiona stopped struggling.

Tall and sleek, a man walked through the haze, black hair whipping around a too-handsome face. He approached and came to a halt before her, gazing down with an expression of amused pity. "Fiona," Emuirdane said, his cultured voice thick with disdain. "Don't you know by now that you aren't strong enough?"

He kneeled to rake a clawed finger over her cheek but did nothing to save her from the pit of jewels. "That you never have been?"

"Please," she begged, hating the tremble in her voice, proof of the very weakness he'd accused her of. She was slipping down, down, deep into a shimmering abyss. "Give me one more chance. I'll find the Ceffyl. I'll bring it back to you."

His laughter was a cruel taunt. "It's far too late for that." Inches from her face, his fingers curled. "You held the artifact in your hands." With a snarl, he shook his fists. "In your hands!"

Black eyes burning, Emuirdane jerked to his feet, shoving a shiny black boot down on top of her head. "You had one simple task, but you were too incompetent to hold on."

"Don't!" she cried, clawing at his foot. She could feel the jewels crush around her ribs.

But the dark Fae ignored her pleas, forcing her under with a strength she couldn't combat. "You let it go, Fiona." He pressed harder. "You let it all go."

She opened her mouth to scream but had no voice, choked silent by the gems gouging her throat.

In the distance, a bell began to ring, so loud it seemed to rattle her brain. Ignoring the sound, she fought desperately to stay above the surface. To stay alive.

But she sank below, and everything went black.

With a jolt Fiona sat upright and gasped for air. She clasped a hand to her neck, blinded by panic.

After a moment her surroundings crystallized. She was in her own bed, safe at home. Sunbeams slanted across her bright, cheery quilt.

But the chill of ghostly fog still slithered on her skin.

The ringing erupted again and she flinched, but the noise grounded her in a welcome reality. One with no Emuirdane and no final death knell.

Just the household phone and a really bad dream.

Throwing back the covers, she dropped bare feet to the cool hardwood floor and rushed out to the hallway. Atop a Hepplewhite table sat a green rotary, the landline her grandfather refused to replace.

She hugged herself against the Bar Harbor cold and snatched up the receiver, cutting off the next ring. "Whiteburn residence."

A deep voice filled her ear, an older man who identified himself as Pete Walsh. Caught off guard and still half-asleep, Fiona listened, thinking he must be a friend of her grandfather's.

But then he spoke of his farm and mentioned one of the fliers her family had left in various towns. The reason for his call registered.

Adrenaline blasted her system. Now she was wide awake.

Fingers tight on the phone and nerves tingling down her arms, she felt her heart kick into a full gallop. She inhaled to slow the rhythm and regain her balance, unable to believe what she was hearing.

Thank you. Thank you. Thank you.

"You found it," she whispered, her voice almost breaking as relief surged.

"Ayuh," the man answered. He had a no-nonsense way about him and asked when she would be available.

"Now," she sputtered. "I can come right away." She rifled through a drawer for pen and paper, though she doubted she'd forget the address. "Where are you located?"

She told herself she should call Tate and Sami. Her sisters were as involved as she was and had every right to know.

But Sami was holed up in her farmhouse in the country, preparing for an art show.

And Tate would be with Jack, enjoying a newlywed bliss Fiona was hesitant to disturb.

After jotting down the instructions, she caught her reflection in the mirror above the table. Running her fingers through the disheveled cap of short black hair, she noted the smudges underneath her eyes, proof of yet another restless night.

Maybe she *should* handle this one by herself. It didn't take Freud to decode the nightmare she'd just had, or the similar versions that had plagued her sleep for the last few months.

Ever since her return.

Emuirdane was more than a monster from a dream, and his threat to those she loved drew closer every day. Dangerous and powerful, the dark Fae remained unsatisfied.

And it was all Fiona's fault.

So no, she wouldn't waste another minute, not even to alert her sisters. This was her opportunity to make things right and redeem herself for past failures.

This was her chance to prove her worth.

Still staring in the mirror, she squared her shoulders and steeled her voice. "I'm on my way."

A mailbox in the shape of a small white house marked the drive, just as Pete Walsh had said it would. Fiona turned onto a lane framed by Aspen trees, their white trunks stark against a winter blue sky.

As her SUV and the trailer she hauled crunched over gravel, she cracked her window to smell the crisp, clean air. At home she had an endless ocean view and the constant lullaby of crashing waves, but the island's interior offered its own type of serenity, its own kind of peace.

Boreal forests ran thick with red spruce and balsam fir, while boulders dotted the ground, carpeted green by moss and lichen. Lush and enchanting, the woodlands were like those of a fantasy faerie land.

And she would know.

Despite the charming scenery of the drive, her anxiety spiked when the house came into view. Her fingers tracked to the scar on her chest, the one she'd received during a near-death-cretid encounter.

In real life. Not just her dreams.

The scar served as a memento from her treacherous time in Faerie, and a reminder that some dangers could find her here too.

Shoving thoughts of Emuirdane aside, she took a final draw on her courage, parked the SUV at the end of the drive, and exited in front of a larger version of the mailbox. The two-story home sported white clapboard with navy-blue shutters, surrounded by dogwoods that were now bare but would bloom a soft pink or white come the spring.

As soon as she got out, a man with wheat-blond hair stepped onto the covered porch. "Ms. Whiteburn?" he greeted in a smooth, clear voice—definitely not the man she'd spoken to on the phone. That one had sounded much older.

"Yes. I'm Fiona Whiteburn." She zipped her fleece to her throat, protection from the biting wind that raced unencumbered across an open pasture. "I'm looking for Mr. Walsh."

He hooked a thumb over his shoulder. "My uncle is in the stables." Long legs carried him to the bottom of the steps where he offered a hand and a kind smile. "I'm Tyler. I saw your flier about the lost horse yesterday when I stopped at a tack and farm store in Holden."

"I'm so glad you did. We've been posting them for months and were beginning to lose hope."

"I'll put your mind at ease and tell you that your horse has been here a while, sheltered and cared for."

Fiona felt a slight give and release beneath her heart, relief that the animal hadn't suffered through the harsh winter. Mount Desert Island was comprised of one hundred and eight square miles, including Acadia National Park. From cobble beaches to mountains and woodlands, the vast wilderness held far too many places for a horse to disappear, to come to harm.

"Uncle Pete never goes to town in the cold months," Tyler continued. "He prefers to play the hermit out here, has his groceries and other necessities delivered. I come out to work with him every spring and summer and just arrived yesterday. He'd told me about this beautiful white horse, so when I saw the flier . . ." He ended with a shrug.

"You made the connection," Fiona said with a smile. "I can't tell you how grateful my family is to you and your uncle for finding our horse." *Especially since I'm the one who lost it.*

She cleared her throat and tried to ban the negativity. "We also insist on reimbursing him for the cost of boarding."

Tyler lifted his hands in mock surrender. "That's something I'll let you take up with the boss." He crooked his head. "Come on back and we'll find him."

Together they rounded the house and headed toward a long wooden building, a typical stable structure with a row of windows down the side. Today they were all shut against the weather, often described this time of year as "soggy and foggy."

Tyler pulled open a door and warm air embraced them, scented with the tangy smell of hay and livestock. "Looks like they're getting some exercise now," he said, gesturing to the far end of the stables where two doors were flung wide.

Beyond them, a man in a camel-hued cowboy hat leaned on the

fence of a circular paddock. But Fiona's gaze traveled past him, her interest solely for the magnificent creature prancing around the yard.

The horse gleamed pure white in the sun, head held high and cantering proudly. The Jeweled Ceffyl, alive and well, and moving with such dignified grace that Fiona's breath caught in her chest.

As if aware of her presence, the animal turned in a small circle and came to a halt. Brown eyes stared directly at Fiona and, even from a distance, evinced gentleness and trust.

"Uncle Pete," Tyler called out beside Fiona, jarring her from the trance.

In response, the older man turned around. Spying the two of them, he lifted a hand in acknowledgment and began a slow amble toward them.

Fiona started to move as well, but a loud neigh drew her attention. A huge black horse stretched his neck over the lower door of its stall, straining in his attempt to gain her notice. Three times, he tossed his nose into the air, clearly beckoning her over.

With a laugh, she eased closer. "Hello, handsome." He was so big, she guessed he had to be male. She took another step and lifted her hand, then stopped to glance at Tyler. "May I?"

"Of course." He leaned a shoulder against the wooden beam next to the stall. "This is Dante."

Amused and charmed by the flirtatious horse, Fiona tentatively caressed his nose, black like velvet and just as soft. A few more strokes and the animal blew out a sound of pure pleasure.

"He likes you."

Dante snuffled in agreement and Fiona's grin widened. "I like him too. It's impossible not to."

"Yeah." Tyler pulled a golden apple from his pocket, slicing the treat into quarters. "This poor guy's going to be heartbroken when you leave, though."

"Why?" Fiona asked, extracting her hand, only to have Dante

reach out for her again.

"He's developed quite a crush on your girl."

Fiona was too involved with the insistent stallion to catch Tyler's meaning. "My girl?" she echoed.

A heavy silence followed.

Fiona realized her mistake and jerked her head toward Tyler. His confused expression confirmed her slip-up.

"Is your horse a male?" he asked. "Because if so, I'm afraid you're about to be disappointed." He shifted his eyes to his approaching uncle who had reached them at last.

"Disappointed why?" Pete Walsh asked, his voice as gruff as she'd remembered, as if whiskey and cigars were lifelong friends.

Fiona clamped down on jitters that wanted to surface and faked what she hoped was an easy laugh. Smile firmly in place, she told Tyler, "I was just surprised you didn't know her name. Then again, how would you?"

Tyler visibly relaxed. "True. That's why we've just been calling her Girl, for lack of a better name. Anyway, once you name them, it's easier to get attached. That's when they take a piece of you with them."

Tyler's words seemed to hit home for Pete, who cast a sad glance toward the paddock where the mare still trotted. Fiona melted a little inside. She wouldn't have taken the gruff older man for such a softy.

"So," Pete cleared his throat, "what's her name?"

Fiona's mind flashed back to when Tate had first lifted the silver horse from its mystical container. How its many jewels had shimmered with magick. "Jewel," she said, and knew immediately it felt right.

Pete nodded. "Well, that sure fits, because she's a high-class gal." He passed between her and Tyler to scratch behind Dante's ear. "I'm glad she's going back home, but we sure are going to miss her." His sigh ruffled the black tuft of hair on the horse's forehead.

"Aren't we, boy?"

Something that might have been guilt tugged at Fiona, making her feel like a con artist come to trick and cajole, taking the mare from a loving home. But wasn't that exactly what she was doing?

She shook off the sensation and considered the alternative. Essentially, there was none.

If she wanted to save her family from Emuirdane's wrath, this was her only option. She had to leave here with the Ceffyl.

No, an inner voice chastised, unwilling to let her be emotionally distant from what was still a living creature. Because she wasn't just walking away with the Ceffyl statuette today.

She was leaving here with *Jewel.*

"I'll be happy to send her with you." Pete slid his eyes to Fiona. "But, as I'm sure you understand, we'll need to review her papers first."

Panic flared a bright, shrieking red behind her eyes, but she couldn't let the two men sense her alarm. A big smile fixed on her lips, she nodded. "Of course."

Her mind, however, continued to race. Why hadn't she thought of that? Why hadn't any of them?

Because she and her family weren't typically horse people, that's why. And cats and dogs rarely required proof of ownership.

Fiona rubbed the base of her throat as anxiety blocked her airway. *What am I going to do now? I shouldn't have tried to handle this by myself.* She thought of saying she'd left the documents at home, but the idea of walking away and leaving Jewel here made her skin feel tight.

She couldn't say why, but her witchy-sense was tingling. And for reasons she couldn't name, she peered over her shoulder, looking for . . . for what?

Dante chose that moment to nudge her, brazen in his need for attention. The horse wasn't shy about getting what he wanted. His black eyes bored into Fiona, strangely mesmerizing, almost hypnotic.

As if he had her *under his spell.*

An idea struck and Fiona stilled. Keeping her eyes on him, she used Dante as a diversion, too ashamed to glance at either of the men as she worked out the details in her head.

She *did* have tools at her disposal, very special skills that could help get her out of this unscathed. And while she'd never turned her powers on innocent bystanders, this was a unique situation. Lives were at stake.

To her way of thinking, that tipped the scales of her conscience toward justified.

Fiona bit her lip and accepted the inevitable. Whether she liked it or not, her magick might be the only answer.

"I'll go get her ready," Pete said, giving Fiona a pat on the arm as he left. The gesture piled on additional weight, tipping those scales back toward guilt.

I'm not going to hurt them, she argued internally, stroking Dante's nose and assuring herself she wasn't a terrible person. *What harm could a tiny, little persuasion spell do?*

Tyler gave her another boy-next-door grin and her stomach looped.

She continued petting Dante as if her life depended on it. *They'll never even realize they were charmed.* Plus, she and her sisters had a rightful claim to the horse.

At least, here in the mortal world, since any others had been left far, far behind. The distance of one dragon ride and one inter-dimensional portal. If she wanted to be specific.

Fiona blocked the disturbing memory—the memory of *him*—and met Tyler's eyes again. He was leaning forward as if trying to get her attention.

"I'm sorry," she said. "Did you say something?"

"I asked if you wanted to step into the office and have some coffee."

She jumped on the excuse. "I'd love coffee." And it would give her time to remember the words to that spell.

When first learning to work enchantments, she'd decided to use Romanian or Welsh, so the magick of her bloodlines would strengthen the effect. So that meant she should try *convinge* . . . or maybe *perswadio*.

"It will be more comfortable in here." Tyler stopped in front of a closed door. "Uncle Pete will get Jewel ready to go." He opened the door and did an "after you" gesture with his hand. "I'll take a look at your papers while we wait."

Her eyes popped wide before she could stop herself. She thought she'd have at least a few more minutes to prepare, but she needed the spell. And she needed it *now*.

Before she could think of a way to stall, a man's voice called out from across the stables. "Did you say papers?"

Chills of recognition ran down Fiona's spine, and the entire world shrunk down to a pinpoint of black. *He can't be here. It's not possible.*

The deep voice belonged to the one person she'd hoped never to lay eyes on again, and even now, she couldn't bear the idea of facing him. Her body, unfortunately, acted on autopilot, turning her around without her permission.

Haloed by daylight flooding in the door, he was nothing but a dark silhouette. But Fiona didn't need to see his face. The warrior's build and aggressive stance were forever burned into her memory.

Finally, he stepped into the light. "I've got the papers right here." Golden-brown eyes found Fiona and raked over her, the scrutiny so intense it heated her skin.

She backed away, shaking her head, as if she could deny his existence and make him disappear.

When she bumped into Tyler, he put a protective hand on her shoulder. "Do you know him?" he asked.

But Fiona didn't answer. She couldn't speak. Not with her pulse slamming in her throat and stomach in a painful twist.

Oh, yes. She knew him. She would never forget him.

"Ronan," she whispered.

The man who'd tried to kill her.

2

Fiona's face turned a terrified white, and pure pleasure warmed Ronan's blood. His heart hammered, pulsing with retribution, the steady thrum pounding out a single accusation again and again.

Thief-Thief-Thief

After all these months, there she stood. The woman—the witch—who'd taken everything from him. Shock and horror were stamped across her delicate features, but he could summon no sympathy.

Not this time.

The Whiteburn sisters deserved no quarter for what they'd done, no mercy whatsoever.

They'd violated a hallowed shrine and stolen something sacred, something that *did not* belong to them. Their appearance and demeanor had duped him once but now, Ronan knew, they embodied all he despised, in humans and Fae alike.

And he'd known some pretty wicked Fae.

Drawing on reserves of calm, he remembered why he'd come and what he must accomplish. With a deep breath, he started toward Fiona, but halted when the man beside her made a move.

Positioning himself in front of her, the blonde man stood tall with his shoulders thrown back. "Can I help you?" he barked out.

The smile curving Ronan's lips could never be mistaken for friendly, but he reminded himself of Fiona's wiles and that the man couldn't really be faulted. Hardwired to follow his instinct, he was just fulfilling a natural role. A male primed to defend the innocent.

Though Fiona Whiteburn was anything but.

Fiona peeked over the other man's shoulder, as if she needed his protection, and Ronan's skin crawled with disgust. *Play your games, little witch. I know who you really are.*

There'd been a time when he'd felt the same inclination as the posturing man, the same need to care for the *gentle* woman. When Fiona's big green eyes had lured him away from reason. When her sweetness and fragility had made him a fool.

One look at her in the Ruins of Morogost, and something deep inside him had shifted. He'd gone against a lifetime of training, breaking protocol and veering from his mission. Even knowing who she was and why she'd come to Faerie, he'd treated her wound and saved her life.

For her—*only* for her—he had chosen mercy.

A choice that had led to his greatest shame.

"I've come for the mare," he said, louder than he'd intended, rage threading his words like the sharpest needle.

The man's eyes narrowed in response, so Ronan made another attempt to reel in his temper. He reminded himself to be cordial, since it would do no good to rile the person currently in possession of the Ceffyl.

He relaxed his rigid muscles and put a less . . . *hostile* expression on his face. He gave the guy a grin that was downright affable and strolled toward him—intentionally ignoring Fiona—to offer his documents for inspection.

"Ronan Gates," he introduced himself, the cheer in his voice enough to make him cringe. "I think you'll find these are in perfect order."

The man didn't give a name in return, his furrowed brow conveying clear distrust. He frowned, but grudgingly accepted the papers. Once he took the time to look them over, his expression morphed to one of confusion. "Fiona," he said at last, turning to her, "I don't understand."

Her pale face blushed a pretty pink. "I'm sorry, Tyler. I . . ."

She trailed off, shamefaced, and Ronan found her embarrassment to be as pleasing as her fear.

"She doesn't have any proof that she owns the horse." He crossed his arms and tried not to sound condescending. A feat he didn't quite pull off. "Ms. Whiteburn is under the impression the mare should be hers." He waved a hand at the documents. "You can see for yourself," he turned his glare on Fiona, "how *wrong* she is."

Tyler studied the certificate and proof of insurance, as well as a printed photo of Ronan with the horse. The picture was real, but the papers had been faked. Such things were not needed in Ronan's world.

Finally, Tyler shifted uncomfortably. "I need to let my uncle read these." Mouth thin with displeasure, he started to leave, but then he hesitated, tossing a concerned glance from Fiona to Ronan.

"Don't worry," Ronan said, eyes and smile tight with feigned goodwill. "I mean the lady no harm. I've just traveled a long way to claim what's rightfully mine."

With a terse nod, Tyler left them, his boots *thunk-thunking* against the wooden floor as he hurried to tell his uncle.

Alone with Fiona, Ronan ground his teeth together and tried to live up to his own vow. That he would be disciplined and calm where she was concerned, spelling out the situation in no uncertain terms. He would be logical, practical, and totally devoid of emotion.

That's what he told himself.

Until he looked at her.

Green eyes sparking with fury, she lifted her chin in a show of bravery. But the pulse fluttering in her neck betrayed her fear, and Ronan couldn't contain a predatory smile.

She crossed her arms, leaning back slightly, but she didn't

retreat. "So you've come to finish the job," she said, shooting him a mutinous look.

As if *he* were the villain in this scenario.

He rounded on her and enjoyed watching her squirm. "I've come to fulfill my duty, if that's what you mean."

She flitted a glance toward the open stable doors where Tyler had vanished. "You won't kill me here, not in front of two witnesses."

"Kill you?" Ronan chuckled and clicked his tongue. "No. Sadly, I missed my opportunity for that in Faerie. If I'd only let you succumb to the cretid's poison, then none of this would be necessary."

She sucked in a breath, her body going rigid. "So you *do* want me dead."

How was he supposed to answer that? He should *want* to murder her, and he certainly had every right. But even now, after all she'd done, the thought of ending her life made his gut roll in revolt.

So all he said was, "I'm not here to kill you, Fiona." Besides, even if he could stomach the idea, there was no way he could take her life. Not now.

"I'm not sure I believe you," she said.

Ronan did nothing to further allay her fears but turned to stare down the stable corridor, watching for Tyler and the uncle he'd spoken of. In a stern tone he told her, "All I can say is that things are much more complicated now."

He heard her feet shuffle, a slow intake of breath, and finally she asked, "How could things possibly be more complicated than before?"

He whirled on her, and this time she did step back. "All you need to concern yourself with is the fact that I've caught up with you and your sisters. I've come to claim the Jeweled Ceffyl and take her back home where she belongs. Where she was *safe*."

Fiona flinched, the tiniest bit, but her expression remained stoic.

"And I will do whatever it takes to stop you."

Ronan sensed her response, the stir of magick in the air, even before her palms glowed a bright, warning white.

But her show of power only hardened his resolve. "Fire, Fiona? In a wooden building filled with hay? Are you so callous that you would endanger the lives of innocent animals? Not to mention Tyler and his uncle who would surely try to save them."

Her flames flickered and died instantly, her brow creasing. "No, I . . ."

"But why should I be surprised? I know you won't let anyone or anything stand in your way."

"That's not true."

Before she could further argue her innocence, he stepped in and crowded her, daring her to move. "Your previous actions prove otherwise."

Contrition slid over her features, but Ronan wasn't through with her yet. He would have pressed her harder, venting some of the resentment he'd stored up these last months, if not for the eruption of a man's voice outside.

"Whoa, whoa!" someone yelled.

Ronan and Fiona turned together as Tyler rushed past the open doors, followed by an older man, presumably the uncle. The two disappeared from sight, and Ronan ran to see what was happening, with Fiona right on his heels.

But before they made it to the end of the building, the white-haired man marched in through the doors, his face red and a hat clenched in his hand. "I don't know what in hell's going on with you two," he shook the hat at them, "but if I find out you've abused that animal, I'll call every authority I know down on your heads. You *will* be held accountable."

"Abused?" Fiona pressed a hand to her stomach. "No."

"Now wait a minute—" Ronan began.

"No, you wait." The grizzled old cowboy cut him off. "That sweet girl has been tame as a kitten and happy here for months, but the minute you two show up she gets skittish. You start arguing, and she becomes terrified."

The older man brought his hands together across his chest, then spread them wide in a slashing motion. "Neither of you is getting that horse today."

"You have no legal right to keep her," Ronan said.

"Keep her?" The man snarled his contempt. "When you two started in at each other, she jumped the paddock. So your papers, Mr. Gates, are worthless. Because she's *gone*."

"Gone?" Fiona lurched past the older man but stopped when she saw Tyler round the corner. He locked eyes with her and shook his head.

Ronan and Fiona sent each other accusing glances.

Fiona took a shuddering breath as if to rail at him, but instead, she made a sound of disgust and muttered to herself, "I've got to find her."

Hands curled into white-knuckled balls, she whirled away, pausing only long enough to tell Pete and Tyler, "I'm sorry for all of this, but I promise you we never hurt her."

With that, she sprinted toward the door that led back to the main house.

With no time to explain or persuade, Ronan turned from the two men.

He had to catch Fiona.

"Hey." Tyler's voice boomed through the narrow building.

Ronan stopped to spare him a glance.

The man was no longer simply posturing, and Ronan felt sure distance was all that kept Tyler from throwing a punch. "What's going on here?"

Ronan gave him his back, planning to ignore him.

But Tyler's harsh voice brought him up short again. "Mr. Gates."

Ronan gave him the courtesy of facing him.

"I don't know what this is," Tyler said, "but when it comes to the horse and the lady, I'd advise you to tread gently."

Ronan held the man's furious stare but offered no reply. The Ceffyl he would always protect, and he had no intention of hurting Fiona.

But treading gently? Well, that was a promise he wasn't prepared to make.

Without another word, he rushed from the stables, catching up with her as she was opening the door of her SUV. Ronan grabbed her by the elbow.

She jerked free. "Don't touch me!"

Ronan released her arm but pinned her with a glare. "We need to talk."

"I have nothing to say to you, and even if I did, there's no time. I have to go find Jewel." She tried to slip into the car.

"No." Ronan blocked her. "You don't."

"Don't try to mislead me like you did in Faerie. I know *exactly* who you are and what you're capable of." She stepped back, lifting both hands. Twin flames of white fire snapped to life in her palms. "How is it you show up now? Today? The very *hour* that I find the horse?"

Ronan remained silent and let her come to her own conclusion. When she did, her eyes flared. "You've been spying on me."

He lifted a shoulder. "Not just you."

The flames leapt and her voice lashed. "I'm warning you now. Stay away from my family."

Ronan clenched his jaw, blocking the heated response that jumped to his tongue. He chose his words carefully, but they still held a bite. "In case you've forgotten, I saved your life in Faerie. I saved all of you from the horde of cretids at the ruins. After that, I gave Tate fair warning of the dangers to come. I even offered to help you all return home."

He felt a tic near his eye but kept going. "All you had to do to keep the peace was leave the Ceffyl where she belonged."

Fiona growled a sound of frustration but seemed to relent, curling her fingers to smother her magick. She reached for the door handle, but he locked a hand onto her wrist.

This time he wasn't letting go, not until she heard him out. "You and your sisters brought the consequences on yourselves."

"Consequences?" she spat. "Dropping us hundreds of feet to our deaths? That's what you call a consequence?"

"I acted only in defense of the Ceffyl." Tightening his grip, he tugged her closer. "I don't think you can say the same."

Her brows clenched, two raven's wings coming together. "You don't know anything."

"Then explain it to me." Ronan held her gaze, searching the depths for any sign that he'd been wrong. That she wasn't like all the rest, those who'd used the horse for their own selfish purposes.

"Why do you want the Ceffyl?" he demanded, though he doubted she could say anything that would make him understand.

She pressed her lips together, evading his question by posing one of her own. "What did you mean before? Why did you say I don't have to find Jewel?"

Ronan didn't like giving away his advantage, but he had to come clean with her. Like it or not, he needed something from her. "I can find the horse whenever I need to." He paused, knowing he was about to show his hand. "I can summon her."

Her stunned gaze flashed to his face and held there, as if searching for any hint of betrayal. "If that's true, then why wait all this time? Why did you follow me here today if you could have already taken her back to Faerie?"

He stood still, watching, and could practically hear her mind working it out.

She found the answer and her face lit up. "Because you can't. You can't change her without the jewels." She choked off a laugh. "And we have them."

The gems are only half of it. Ronan finally took his hand away, trying to decide how much to tell her. "As much as it pains me to admit, you and I need each other."

"I don't need anything from you." She tilted up her face in defiance. "I found Jewel once. I'll find her again."

"Fine." *Foolish witch.* "I suppose you know how to change her back?" Ronan was certain she didn't know the first step. Because he didn't either.

Fiona stared at him for a beat, and then another. "You could be lying."

"But I'm not." Ronan leaned against the door of the vehicle, effectively keeping her where he wanted her. But he made sure not to touch her again, since the hand he'd held her with was still uncomfortably warm from the memory of her skin.

"I'm offering you a truce, Fiona. But I offer it only once." He drew out the pause. "And *only* to you."

She angled her head at him, scrutinizing.

"We work together to find the Ceffyl and return her to her inanimate state."

She made a strange sound in her throat. "You think I would help you? After you bombed a bridge from beneath my feet? After you tried to kill my sisters? And Brit and Jack?"

"Consequences, Fiona." His easy tone belied the wrath firing to life inside. "And yes, you will cooperate. Because whether you want to admit it yet or not, you need me. I'm the only one who can find the Ceffyl."

He walked away from her, making it clear she was free to go. "If you refuse, you'll never see the horse again. I'll take her off this island and halfway across the world. Anything to protect her. To keep her away from people like you."

She grunted as if offended, but Ronan couldn't find it in himself to care. If she didn't like his opinion of her, it was up to her to change it.

"If you take her," she said, "you won't be able to change her back."

"At least she'll be safe from those who would exploit her." Those who would use her, taking what they wanted without remorse or any thought of the repercussions.

Fiona nibbled on her lower lip as if considering her options.

The action drew Ronan's notice to her pretty bow of a mouth, and at once he grew disgusted with himself. He let that revulsion work for him, reinforcing his threat with a hard tone and yet another ultimatum. "Don't tell your family I'm here or what happened today."

Her jaw went slack.

"That's non-negotiable."

When her jaw clenched but she kept quiet, Ronan knew he had her.

"I need to go," she said, averting her eyes. "I need to think."

"Fine. You have until tomorrow." Ronan withdrew a business card from the pocket of his jeans. "I'm staying here. Room's on the back."

She said nothing, just glared at his extended hand. At last, she stepped forward and accepted the card. Then she climbed into the car and slammed the door, one last display of vexation.

Ronan could do nothing more, so he watched her wheel around and speed down the drive. Her tires spun, spewing gravel against the trailer she hauled with a rapid-fire *tink-tink-tink*.

The woman was obstinate, tenacious beyond reason.

And it was that staunch persistence that circled him back to his own questions. The ones that had burned in his mind for months.

Why were Fiona and her family willing to risk their lives in pursuit of the Ceffyl?

What in all the worlds could make them want the horse so badly?

3

Castle Sangridor
The Ielonaar Realm

Dusk was a crimson warning on the horizon when Emuirdane materialized within the obsidian walls of King Malrik's castle. Merciless winds thrashed his cloak against his body as he scanned the forbidding environment.

Along the castle's outer wall, sharp spikes rimmed the parapets, and murder holes lined the battlements. As if these deterrents weren't enough, vipera perched atop each corner tower, fierce lookouts ready to devour any foolish trespassers.

The great winged creatures were red and black, bred over time to bear Malrik's signature colors. Positioned at the forefront in every battle, the dragons filled enemies with awe, a far more terrifying banner than any simple flag.

Equally bleak and desolate was the landscape surrounding the castle. Black jagged mountains stood on every side, unforgiving and inaccessible terrain. Hidden tunnels led inside the kingdom, but only those who served the warrior king were privy to their secrets.

Emuirdane grinned slyly to himself, for he need not travel beneath the earth, nor across the sky. His magick allowed him access to wherever he wished, within this world, and even to that of the mortals.

A fact his adversary greatly resented.

Malrik Sangridor had an insatiable need to ruin and rule, to murder and maim. A warrior first and king second, he'd invaded almost every other empire in the realm. Few territories had escaped the bite of his blade, mostly those located in the farthest reaches.

Emuirdane's lands were safe as well, due only to the tenuous truce they shared. A truce based on a long-standing contract, and one that was nearing its expiration.

With a long breath to steady a sudden bout of nerves, Emuirdane glanced up at the two moons. The twin blue orbs crept ever closer.

Time was running out.

Still, he must brandish his fortitude and conceal his concerns. He mustn't show doubt or worry, reveal no sign of weakness or fear. Not within the foul halls of Sangridor Castle.

So with his head held high, he sauntered up the wide stone steps and into a massive chamber lined by pillars of onyx. He strolled across black tiles streaked with crimson until he reached the arched entryway leading to the throne room.

He allowed the hulking guards to open the doors and entered. Cloaked in an air of superiority, he made his way to the raised dais.

Seated on his granite throne, King Malrik offered no word of welcome, nor any gesture of hospitality. He only fixed his guest with a steely glare, his pitch-dark eyes flashing a deep and bloody red.

A frisson of unease crawled down Emuirdane's neck. How he hated Malrik's eyes. The revolting mark of *his kind.*

"Emuirdane." His name rolled like thunder from the warmongering king. "To what do I owe the honor of your presence?" Sarcasm dripped from Malrik's words, and the corner of his mouth notched up almost imperceptibly.

Emuirdane sniffed, refusing to show emotion, but the green stones in his ring and matching brooch churned and swirled. His magick responded to the affront though he dared not. "I bring news of the Jeweled Ceffyl," he said, words clipped and brusque.

Malrik remained mute, one haughty black brow winging upward.

Spine stiff, Emuirdane gave a false smile and played his part. This baseborn cur had never shown him his due respect, and while Malrik's physical prowess might rival his own strength in magick, the two kings were most emphatically *not* equals.

"The youngest of the sisters located the Jeweled Ceffyl today." Unwilling to even flinch, Emuirdane held the other's hard stare. "Unfortunately, the horse fled."

A heavy sigh flowed from Malrik, and he tapped one finger on an armrest. "So you've clouded my halls with news of another failure."

Emuirdane's ego could not let the statement pass. "I have *not* failed." He did his best to look down his nose at the man seated above. "The witch *will* find the animal again. My oracle has assured me of this." He didn't blink at the lie he told. The crone who served as his seer had reported Fiona's activities but could not predict future events.

If so, he would demand to know the fate of the Legion warrior, the man called Ronan, a most unexpected and unwelcome development. The man had no business in the human world.

For now, he was little more than a bothersome pest, as Emuirdane held more sway over Fiona than this uninvited guest. Still, he couldn't risk the man influencing the witch's decisions or stoking some misguided compassion for the animal she pursued.

A small inconvenience, yes, but one that needed to be dealt with.

"There's been a slight complication," he told Malrik, withholding the specifics or mention of the warrior.

"Another one?" The king's tone was bored. "I find myself tiring of your innumerable excuses."

"Fine. If you feel you can obtain the artifact in your own way ..." Emuirdane let the taunt hang in the air. If the king had any other options, he would have made use of them long ago, but neither he nor Emuirdane could locate the Ceffyl.

Though no longer in Faerie, the horse's location was still shielded from the hungry eyes of the Iele Fae. Since its creation, the Jeweled Ceffyl was deemed too powerful for such a violent species, and the gods had ensured no Iele could ever find it for themselves.

Only others—like the sisters three—could deliver the statue to one of their kind.

With a grunt, the king snapped his fingers, summoning a servant who carried a silver goblet on a silver tray. No gold here in Ielonaar. Never that deadly poison. "I fulfilled my end of the bargain decades ago," he said gruffly, snatching the cup to take a gulping drink.

Emuirdane caught a glimpse of one sharp fang, and when Malrik spoke again, it was through crimson-stained teeth. "Perhaps I should have held back. If for all these years you had been suffering the same disappointment, the same dissatisfaction as I, you might have found the necessary incentive."

The king licked his lips. "Perhaps," he said, eyes slashing toward Emuirdane, "I should reclaim my payment."

The threat slammed hard into Emuirdane, straight to the center of his chest where it clamped around his heart—and *squeezed*. Once the organ released, pounding painfully against his ribs, he was able to draw a heated breath. "You wouldn't dare," he fumed.

Malrik lifted a lazy shoulder and grinned.

The contract between the two kings forbade them from doing harm to one another, at least until the Stag Moon marked the end of the agreement and the time when all recompense was due.

But the vile king had other ways to deliver punishment.

Arms sheathed within the folds of his cloak, Emuirdane hid his trembling hands.

Still, his rival sensed his agitation and loosed a wicked laugh.

"Be at ease," Malrik crooned, his mocking tone evidence of how much he enjoyed taunting his guest. "I have no interest in taking back what I gave you. It is worthless to me. Always was."

Another loud sigh and he leaned forward in his seat, splaying his fingers to grip the granite armrests of his throne. "However ..."

Silence pounded in the room as a single red drop escaped the corner of his mouth.

"If you fail to deliver the Ceffyl, there is something else you could offer in its stead. Something I covet almost as dearly."

Gaze narrowed, Emuirdane turned his head slightly away. His heart rate slowed, but his suspicion grew. "Why have you never mentioned this before?"

Malrik turned his attention to a long bank of windows, to the two moons hovering in the dark sky. "Never have we been so close to the Stag Moon." His eyes slid back to Emuirdane. "Or had you not realized the time?"

"I do not need reminding."

"Good. Good." The king steepled his fingers. "Only one thing can replace the Ceffyl. Only one thing will I accept in its stead."

"Yes?" Emuirdane flung up an impatient hand.

Malrik gave him a cannibal's smile. "I want your blood."

Stunned, Emuirdane gaped at the other king. Surely he didn't mean ...

His entire body began to quiver, outrage stringing his body as tight as a bow. And this time when his magick roared, so did he. "You would demand a life exchange?" He strode forward. "From *me*?"

Malrik tilted his head. "Ah, Emuirdane, always so arrogant. But even you must obey the laws set down for all Fae kind." He sneered. "Lest you forget, they apply even to *royals*." The last word dripped with hate for those born into status.

In response to the unworthy king's disdain, Emuirdane's pride reared up like a beast. "You dare insult me this way? You? A lowly peasant who murdered his way to the throne?" Power sizzled around him, crackling with unspent destruction.

Malrik stood, his brows clashing. "This from the man who killed his own father for a crown? And let me remind you," he jabbed out a finger, "should you attack, the terms of our contract are void. I will then be free to take your life, your lands, your kingdom, and all that you possess. Including *her*."

Again the threat to what Emuirdane held most dear. Such disrespect would not be borne! Seething, furious, he forced himself to rein in his magick. Like him, it wanted to strike.

It wanted to kill.

But he must find a way to maintain control. The Ceffyl was finally within his reach, far too close to sabotage his victory. Through clenched teeth he said, "I will deliver the Jeweled Ceffyl. I *will* uphold my end of the contract."

"Let us hope so," Malrik said, before adding with a snarl, "or I *will* have your blood."

Unwilling to tolerate any more blasphemy—Take the life of a royal? Profane!—Emuirdane summoned the silver haze that would transport him away from this wretched place.

But as he vanished, he favored Malrik with a conceited smile, taunting the king with a power he would never possess.

Never would that inferior cur have his life. *Never* would he have his blood.

Outraged and affronted, Emuirdane focused on the place he wanted to go, on the world he chose to enter. He would pay a visit to the mortal realm, and once there, he would be rid of the complications.

By eliminating one bothersome pest.

4

Ronan barely made a sound as he traveled the brick walkway of the inn. Ever alert, ever watchful, he moved with the agile strength of the warrior he was, past a gurgling water fountain and into the elegant Tudor-style home serving as his base camp while he stayed on the island.

Damp mists had slipped in to blanket the night, so the wide foyer with rich, dark wood and creamy walls was especially warm and welcoming. Once inside, he exhaled a breath and allowed his usual vigilance to slip away.

Not only was the inn luxurious, but he'd lined the property with his own protection runes. Here, at last, was a place he could truly let his guard down.

With a nod to the clerk on duty, he crossed the foyer, made a turn, and followed the arched hallway down to his room.

"Mr. Gates." The housekeeper, known to him only as Angie, walked toward him with the quick steps that always made her seem busy. "Please let me apologize for the bureau in your room. I went to stock extra linens in the top drawer, but it seems to be stuck."

Ronan pretended surprise. "I haven't noticed." *Because the drawer isn't stuck.* It was spelled to remain closed. His own version of a room safe.

"Our normal handyman's out of town. Gone down to Florida to visit the grandchildren." She smiled at the last, blue eyes sharp and clear below a fringe of silver hair. "But I'll find someone to take a look tomorrow."

"There's really no need," Ronan said, thankful for Florida and the grandkids. It wouldn't do to have someone poking around that drawer. A simple tug from Angie posed no worry, but a determined man with an arsenal of tools?

"Why don't you wait until I check out?" he suggested. "You can set the towels on the bathroom counter for now."

"You sure?" She angled her head.

"Positive." *In fact, I insist.*

With a bob of her head she carried on toward the front, and Ronan turned to enter his room. Inside, the planks of the floor were painted teal and the wallpaper crowded with tiny flowers. But the suite was spacious and served his needs. In addition to the requisite bed and bath, it also offered a desk and couch, with a fireplace to stave off the bitter chill.

Though spring was already knocking on the door, the nights in Bar Harbor still leaned toward cold. Winds off the water could skewer straight to his marrow, especially after long hours spent trolling the area.

Or "spying," as Fiona preferred to say.

He'd light a fire later as he often did, but first he wanted to check on his safe. Moving to the bureau, he put the tip of his finger on the top right corner, precisely where he'd made his mark.

In a slow motion, he traced the rune backwards, essentially undoing the spell. The drawer slid easily over its wooden slides, revealing a bevy of tiny glass vials and orbs nestled in fabric.

The ranks of the Legion consisted solely of human men, but a life in Faerie required magick. In addition to being soldiers, he and his men were chemists—of a sort. Part of their training involved the harnessing of mystical energies, the manipulation and creation of power.

He opened a black box and studied the balls within, their thick glass concealing glowing swirls of gold and silver. Destructive forces waiting to be set free.

Ronan imagined the handyman disturbing these and grimaced. He should have been more cautious, but now he would do better. He'd add a deterrence spell to the entire bureau. Safer to simply keep people away.

Cautiously, he lifted an orb from the velvet lining of the box. Magick tingled in his palm. The flesh of his hand lit up with silver, reminding him of the bridge at Mount Aeylwon where he'd last used this particular weapon.

Unbidden, an image of Fiona rose to his mind.

Again.

He couldn't stop thinking of how she'd reacted to him today, chewing on her bottom lip, her face waxen and pale, exactly how she'd looked so often in Faerie. By all appearances, she'd seemed shaken and afraid.

But he knew better. Dismissing the notion of the witch's frailty, he replaced the explosive orb, closed the drawer on his weaponry, and drew the runes to seal and repel.

He was well aware of Fiona's power and the incredible magick she had inherited. Two bloodlines, Romanian and Welsh, had combined to produce three sisters destined to travel between the worlds and free the Jeweled Ceffyl.

Ronan now bore the stigma of that defeat, of being the only Legion commander to fail in his sacred duty. Yes, the sisters had been prophesied to take the Ceffyl, but for him, that only increased his shame.

Because he'd known they were coming. He'd known when they'd arrived. Still, he'd allowed Fiona to live, had even *ensured* her survival. And if the predictions were true, the Daughters of Nadia would now bring the Legion's era to an end.

But not if he had anything to say about it.

Ronan had sworn to defend the Ceffyl and so he would, even if the foe he battled was Fate itself. Too many before him had upheld their oaths, making great sacrifices to do so. And far too many had died.

For centuries, the Jeweled Ceffyl had been stolen, passed around, and secreted away, just to be stolen all over again and taken to Faerie. But the Fae were a capricious species, already blessed with magick and long life. Thus the wishes they asked for were far more disastrous.

Eventually—after enough destruction and ruin—the ruling Summer and Winter courts had convened a council, decreeing the Ceffyl be guarded. So with the assistance of the gods, a chest of gold and silver was created, an enchanted strongbox to house the artifact.

The chest was secluded high atop Mount Aeylwon, and the Legion was formed in its defense.

Ronan moved to the window and watched the moonlight glinting on the harbor. After so many years battling beings as strong and insidious as the Fae, he was amazed that three mortal women had passed the trials of the mountain, succeeding where so many had failed. And to fail was to perish.

Fiona and her family must be in desperate need of something, a desire so great only the Jeweled Ceffyl could deliver. Ronan had no idea what they could need so badly.

And they had no idea that every wish came with a cost.

Despite everything, he hoped to avoid violence, another reason he'd made a thorough study of the Whiteburn clan. It paid to know one's enemies.

That's why he'd done more reconnaissance after Fiona had left him at the stables, staking out her home from a secluded spot in the forest. The trailer had been returned, but other than her mother and grandfather arriving at the house, there'd been no other sign of activity. He'd waited hours for Fiona to show, but she never had.

Ronan's stomach rumbled, as if prompted by his recall of the long, cold day, so he went to the phone and dialed the front desk. He'd eat in his room tonight and get some rest.

And that way he'd be available. Just in case Fiona called.

After placing his order, he hung up and wondered for the tenth time what she would decide to do, whether or not she'd tell anyone he was here. If his threats worked and she remained silent, his plans would go more smoothly.

One female witch would be much easier to handle than four.

Not to mention the men and all their weapons. The sisters' uncle Brit was a lawyer by trade but could transform into a lethal adversary, especially with his ancient crossbow at his back. And while Tate's new husband Jack didn't have any power as far as Ronan could tell, even giant and poisonous cretids had fallen beneath the man's vellenium axe.

And just where had he gotten his hands on that mystical blade? The metal was rare and highly prized, one of the few things that could kill the immortal Fae.

Magick. Wits. Weapons. The Whiteburns were not a foe to be taken lightly. Even the grandfather was more than he seemed on the surface, never without his long silver cane, yet never actually using it to walk.

Deciding on a drink while he waited for the food, Ronan moved to the bottle of Maker's Mark on the coffee table and poured two fingers' worth in a tumbler. He tossed it back and felt it hit his stomach.

The whiskey burned inside of him, along with his conviction. Prophecy, witches—none of it mattered. Nothing would stop him from completing his mission.

Because his family had a history of its own. Long had Gates men defended the Jeweled Ceffyl, keeping her safe from the greed and corruption of humans and Fae alike.

And damned if he'd be the one to tarnish that legacy.

When the muscles in his shoulders tensed, he rolled off the

stress, began to recap the bottle, and . . . *screw it*. He poured another shot.

The whiskey was halfway to his mouth when a strange illumination drew his eyes to the patio doors. A golden glow filtered through the glass panes. Instinctively, he reached for the *seelion* he kept under the sofa, careful with the curved blade and its lethal edge.

He slid one door open, only to be met by an ocean-scented breeze and a light so bright he saw nothing but the shimmering beams.

Then a figure stepped out of the brilliance. Someone he hadn't expected to meet here. Not in this world.

He bowed his head briefly, then returned his gaze to the powerful being's face. In deference, he lowered his weapon, and waited for instructions.

5

Fog rolled in from the ocean, all but obscuring the curving road ahead of Fiona. Headlights on low, she still recognized the approach to Thunder Hole and reduced her speed accordingly. She was already driving slowly, but the thick white mists could be deceiving, making the twists and turns especially dangerous.

She peered out the passenger window. Beyond the line of evergreens, the land became a barrier of huge, rounded rocks that dropped off into the Atlantic.

With her hands on the steering wheel, she gripped until her knuckles went white. But more was bothering her than eerie weather and treacherous landscape. Regret had stuck with her all day long, clinging to her like rotten vines.

She'd messed up in a spectacular way and had no idea how to fix it.

Not only had she made a huge mistake, she didn't know how, or even what, she was going to tell her family. Should she walk in and announce her rash behavior? That she'd followed her pride and acted on her own, only to end up losing the Jeweled Ceffyl a second time?

That's assuming she told them the truth at all.

The idea of lying scraped her conscience like a rusty knife, but if Ronan meant what he'd said, then she didn't really have a choice. She couldn't afford to make another—no, a *third*—blunder by revealing his presence and losing the horse for good.

If he was the only one who could find Jewel, and he truly would take her far away, then Fiona was forced to keep quiet. Ronan's existence in this realm, in her very hometown, had to be kept a secret.

And, she thought, turning off the song clanging from the radio, she'd also have to cooperate with him. She had the jewels, and he could get the Ceffyl. *Quid pro quo.*

The thought made waves crash in her stomach, even greater than those slamming into the craggy coastline. He'd already tried to kill her and her loved ones, and there was no guarantee he wouldn't try again.

"Ugh!" She smacked the steering wheel with her palm, irritated by the predicament she'd caused. Even the Winter Queen would be a better partner. She'd only attempted to trick Fiona and her sisters in Faerie, not once bombarding them with magickal grenades.

But Ronan had. And this was the man she had to trust? He was so arrogant, so condescending, so . . .

Fiona clenched her jaw and shook away the image of those golden-brown eyes. She grew even more unsettled as she recalled her reaction, how she'd heated and flushed beneath his bold perusal.

Another *thump* with her palm on the steering wheel. "Why would I respond like that?" The self-criticism burst free, and a whole new level of shame swamped her. "He tried to murder me. He followed us home." *Thump. Thump.* "He's been spying on all of us!"

Triple-*thump.*

An aggravated sigh rushed from her lips. She despised him. He was her very worst—okay, second worst—enemy and could ruin everything she and her sisters had struggled to achieve.

So why, she asked the secret part of her heart, why did she care what he thought of her?

People like you, he'd said to her, with so much disdain and scorn she'd almost felt his derision crawl across her skin.

But he didn't know what her family faced. He didn't know they only needed the Ceffyl to ransom off to Emuirdane. If they didn't give the Iele the horse, he'd promised them bloodshed.

She couldn't tolerate the idea of her mother being hurt or taken away again, or Brit, her sisters . . . or Granddad. He was almost seventy, but that wouldn't faze Emuirdane.

Cramps of revulsion wracked her body. Every option was appalling.

And after seeing Jewel today, so graceful, and innocent, and . . . *free*. Fiona felt awful for a whole new reason.

But she couldn't let her too-tender heart call the shots. There was too much at stake.

That's why she could never tell Ronan what they planned to do with the horse. If he knew who they intended to give it to . . . such a powerful artifact in Emuirdane's villainous hands.

Fiona shuddered. "Just suck it up, Fee. You've always known there were no easy answers." She and her family had been strong-armed into this mess, and she didn't owe Ronan an explanation.

Even if that secret part of her heart kind of wanted to give him one.

With a shake of her head, she pictured Sami. She could almost hear her sister's voice. *Fiona the people pleaser.* That's what Sami always called her.

And that's what Fiona always was. All her life, she could never bear for anyone to not like her.

Even a would-be-killer like Ronan.

"I'm pathetic," she thought out loud.

"Pathetic," a deeper voice echoed.

Fiona jumped and almost swerved off the road, jamming the brake pedal to the floor before she lost control.

"Who is it?" she cried, twisting around to search the back seat.

No one was there.

She whipped her head around, double-checking every inch of the car's interior. There was nowhere for a person to hide. So where had the voice come from?

Slowly she scanned the road and forest outside, squinting to discern shapes cloaked by the fog. The tall, dark hemlocks seemed suddenly aggressive, their shadows lengthening as if their limbs were arms, reaching for her.

Mists encroached, crushing in on her from all sides, and the night as a whole seemed more spirited, more alive.

Then something moved within the trees.

Fiona grappled at the steering column to switch on her high beams. Fear climbed up from her chest to clutch at her throat, and her pulse whooshed in her ears like the liquid beat of a sonogram.

Unblinking, she stared at the space where she'd sensed movement, where despite her shining headlamps, a mass of darkness resisted the light. As she watched, the gloomy patch writhed and shivered.

Emuirdane stepped out of the abyss.

Inside her vehicle, Fiona recoiled. Why was he here? Why now? His appearance on the day she'd let the Ceffyl slip away was no coincidence.

And it was no accident he'd stopped her in a place where no one would hear her scream.

"I agree," he said. "You are pathetic." He stood a distance from the vehicle, but his voice resounded as if he were right beside her. "Poor, pitiful, weak Fiona." The Iele made a *tsk-tsk-tsk* sound, mocking her with false sympathy. The length of his black coat flapped against his legs as he crossed his arms and pinned her with his savage stare. Dark as obsidian, his eyes held her in place.

In her lap, Fiona grasped her hands together and squeezed to still the trembling. She should be used to him by now, but she'd never had to face him on her own. For the first time she realized how much she depended on her sisters.

Her magick alone didn't stand a chance.

"What have you done, Fiona?" His voice echoed within the car—within her mind—but still she climbed from the vehicle and took a few unsteady steps in his direction.

"Emuirdane." Her voice sounded too meek, so she took a deep breath and steadied her tone. "What do you want?"

He only shook his head and looked at her with contempt. "You do know why the warrior sought you out, don't you?"

So he was aware of Ronan. Not a surprise. Emuirdane had ways of . . . knowing things. "Let me explain," she said.

"Because you are the weak one. The one he knows he can control." His red lips turned up at the corners. The sadistic Iele enjoyed his petty torments. He thrived on fear.

Fiona balled her hands at her sides, refusing to show how intimidated she felt. "If you'll just listen. I'm close to getting the Ceffyl. I know I'll find it again."

"By yourself?" His laughter hit her like poisoned darts. "You forget how much I know about you. How I've watched over you and your sisters your entire lives, waiting for the day you would be of use to me."

Emuirdane shifted, an eerie figure immersed in the writhing fog and the glow of headlights. "Abandonment syndrome. Isn't that what they called it?"

Fiona gasped involuntarily, as if he'd reached into her with both hands and wrenched something out. "Stop it," she rasped. Barely a command, more like a plea.

Emuirdane's cruel eyes gleamed in the way of a schoolyard bully, one who'd found his prey's soft underbelly. And intended to strike there again and again. "Wretched little orphan. Just a baby when her parents died and left her all alone."

Her head still spun, but she regained her voice. "But my mother didn't die. Your *wife* took her from us."

"Yet you were damaged just the same."

"Why are you doing this?" Her voice broke on the last. She was hungry, distraught, and physically drained. Now this. "You must know I've spent the whole day searching the island. You must have been watching."

For he was always watching.

"Yes, I know of your wasted day." His persona changed abruptly. Gone was the sarcastic mien, the callous smiles. Instead his countenance filled with rage, emerald-hued electricity sparking all around him. "I'm *painfully* aware of the time you have squandered."

He notched up his chin, and a bolt of power streaked over her shoulder. A warning shot.

"But that's not why I'm here. Your continued inadequacy is not what enrages me." He raised his hand, palm upward and fingers curled, a furious ball of lightning barely held in check.

"You are in league with the Legion."

Fiona raised her hands. "I'm not. I swear!"

But her denial went unheard, and Emuirdane speared two jagged bolts into her torso. The force entered her like two flaming swords. They stuck in place and lifted her off the ground.

Fiona could feel her body quaking, she could hear her teeth grinding and her bones groaning as the voltage coursed throughout. She couldn't move, couldn't open her eyes. She could only bear the pain and wait for it to pass.

The current sucked back out of her and she dropped.

But she didn't fall to the road. She was seated upright, back inside her car again.

Emuirdane still stood in her headlights. He flicked a finger, and the engine of her SUV roared to life, revving in a menacing way.

"What—" she began, but her words ended in a small cry when the gearstick shifted into drive. "No!" she shouted, grabbing the lever with both hands. It wouldn't budge. She shoved the brake to the floor and sent a terrified glance to Emuirdane.

The engine still screamed beneath the hood.

"Don't," she whispered, still holding his black gaze.

He gave her a horrible smile.

And let her go.

Tires squealed on the asphalt, and the vehicle shot forward, its raging engine propelling her off the road. The car sliced between two pines, knocking off one of the rearview mirrors.

With a scream locked in her lungs, Fiona pumped the brake, but the car continued to lurch and bump over the ground. Straight toward the sea.

The elevation wasn't as high as the cliffs, but her speed was too fast. She would roll and shatter against the rocky outcropping before dropping into the freezing waters of the Atlantic. Even if she survived the crash, the waves would take her down.

Emuirdane controlled the car, so the brakes were worthless. She couldn't slow down, couldn't stop.

With no other choice, she rolled down her window and prepared to jump. Better to land on gravel and grass than against the rocks, into the ocean, or—she trembled—anywhere near Thunder Hole.

As if the Iele had somehow sensed her plan, the glass got stuck halfway down. Maybe she could still slip out. She had to try.

But then the fog thinned to reveal mountains of stone. "Oh, God." *I'm not going to make it!* She shoved herself through the window but got caught at her hips.

She pushed harder, releasing a sound that was half scream, half sob. She couldn't get free.

The rusty color of rocks filled her peripheral vision just before the SUV glanced off the side of a boulder and vaulted into the air.

Fiona flew from the window as if she'd never been stuck, and for a terrible moment, time seemed to stop. Her body was flung high, up into the cold, dark night, where she floated, weightless.

Too soon, she felt her stomach drop, and the rough surface of a boulder rushed up to meet her. She landed hard against the massive stone, and then—a jolt, numbness, no air.

Stars above shined too brightly, sparkling against the midnight blue. She stared at the specks of white, her mind adrift in a wash of nothingness.

Then agony began a slow crawl through her bones.

A wave crashing close jarred her back to awareness. "I have to move," she mumbled, afraid of being pulled into the roiling black water.

Somehow she'd lived through the crash, but hypothermia would be a more ruthless fate, unless she drowned first.

Or Emuirdane appeared and ended her himself.

She tried to roll over, but pain burst between her shoulder blades. Another wave hit, and splashed her face. She had to get off the rocks.

She made another attempt, pushing with her hands, but something wasn't right.

A horrible realization dawned, and the weight of true terror dropped in her gut. A whimper eased from her lips.

She couldn't roll over. She couldn't sit up.

Because she couldn't move her legs.

6

Fiona blinked her eyes rapidly, wondering what was happening to her as the numbness began to recede from her legs, and the scenery around her began to change. Her vision darkened and blurred, leaving her in a dreamy state, as if she were half-asleep.

But she woke abruptly when a hand patted her on the shoulder. She found herself sitting in the driver's seat of her car once again, with Emuirdane right beside her.

"I don't know about you," he said smugly, "but I quite enjoyed that."

Confusion still a web in her head, Fiona wiggled her toes and—pride be damned—released a sob of relief when they responded.

"Yes, I imagine it was horrifying for you, believing yourself paralyzed." He might have seemed concerned if not for the delight shining in his black eyes. "In fact, this whole experience has changed my mind about killing any of your family."

She jerked her head toward him, hope a tiny flicker in her heart. Could he possibly feel remorse for what he'd just done to her?

"After all, dead is dead." He waved his fingers. "And why should I be content with a single act of vengeance," he leaned in close and whispered, "when I can keep killing all of you in painful and creative ways? Imagine it, Fiona. A new and terrible death, every day, for the *rest of your lives.*"

She could imagine it, too well. Even now, gruesome images flashed in her mind, and the breath shuddered from her lungs.

"It was all a glamour." A type of enchantment at which the Fae excelled, and the next best—or worst—thing to reality.

Except, there were no boundaries. Whatever he wanted to plant in someone's head, they would fully accept. And fully experience.

As she could now attest.

She'd believed it all. Racing through the trees, crashing on the coastline, being flung so hard and fast that she'd struck a huge rock and broken her back. Swallowing hard, she put a hand to her stomach to quiet the rising nausea.

She'd never imagined a glamour being used that way, but now she understood how the power could be abused. And she was terrified for her family.

Cutting her eyes to Emuirdane, she said, "I'll bring you the Ceffyl. Just please don't do this to anyone else."

Forcefully, he gripped her chin and held her face steady. "Then make wise choices concerning that Legion soldier. Swear to me now that you won't give him the Ceffyl, or I might feel inclined to peel Sami's skin from her luscious body."

"I swear!" Fiona burst out. She swallowed but couldn't stop the heave of her stomach. What she'd just suffered through was nothing compared to what he'd just threatened to do to her sister. "I won't give him the Ceffyl."

"Then we understand one another." He snarled the words and released her chin before evaporating into a silver mist.

Alone again, Fiona slumped in her seat. And tried to stop the pictures flashing in her head, images of her family being tortured.

※※※

"There you are," Fiona's mother said, standing at the stove stirring a bubbling orange sauce. "We've been trying to call, but your phone kept going to voicemail."

Fiona took in the scene. Her mother cooking, Tate and Jack

filling glasses with tea, Sami taking dishes down from the cream-colored cabinets, and Brit near the fireplace, deep in discussion with Granddad. It looked like the whole tribe was here.

So much for sneaking in unnoticed.

"Sorry about that." Fiona's smile felt limp, so she tried to infuse more cheer into her voice. "My battery must be dead." She should have known better than to come in through the kitchen, but she'd wanted to double-check the horse trailer to see if it looked exactly how her uncle had left it two days before.

Caught unaware by the gathering, she turned away from her family—hoping none of them noticed her shaking hands or strained expression—and stepped into the mudroom to hang up her jacket and gather her wits. She channeled calm and thought about her mother, who was clearly happy to have the whole family together.

Fiona didn't want to spoil her joy, and neither did she want to raise suspicion. So that meant she'd better get her act together and pretend nothing was out of the ordinary. That everything was normal.

Well, as normal as they could possibly be where the Whiteburns were concerned.

Bone-weary and sick to her stomach after dealing with Emuirdane, Fiona closed her eyes. If anyone asked about her disquiet, she'd tell them she was exhausted. Which wasn't a lie.

It just wasn't the whole truth either.

When she walked back in, Sami was setting the long wooden table. "Family dinner," she said, holding up a plate. "I was too tired to cook, so I called and surreptitiously planted the idea in Mom's head."

Their mother rolled her eyes, the same gypsy-brown as Tate's and Sami's. "If by surreptitious you mean begging me to make Romesco sauce, then sure, you were so sly I hardly noticed your devious plan. Actually, I'm pretty sure this was all *my* idea."

"I'm sure it was," Tate chimed in. Then to Sami, "And how could you be too tired when your usual fare consists of a microwave dinner? Or," she added, "a trip to the sub shop if you're really feeling like a gourmet meal."

Sami just shook her head, jostling the riot of reddish-brown curls tied back in a messy bun. "Even you can't get to me tonight, Tate. I feel too damn good to take part in sibling rivalry."

Fiona tensed automatically, accustomed to the bickering that had been a long-standing tradition between her older sisters. But when Tate cocked her head and grinned, she knew she was overreacting. Being too sensitive.

Because that was *her* long-standing tradition.

Paused in the middle of pouring tea into a glass, Tate eyed Sami. "Are you saying this is a celebration dinner?"

Sami set the last plate down and shrugged. "Maybe if—oh, I don't know—if I happened to have finished the underwater piece today."

"Oh!" their mother cried, just as Tate put the tea pitcher down and rushed to give Sami a hug.

Realizing she was still as taut and strained as a stretched wire, Fiona popped off an excited "Yay!" and hurried to join in the congratulations. All the while she chanted to herself, *Act normal. Act normal. Act normal.*

But even with all the hugging, her face felt like a porcelain mask, one that might shatter any moment if she maintained the fake smile. So she asked a question to keep everyone's attention on Sami's news. "Will you use the new piece in the show?"

"You bet your little cinnamon buns I will." Sami sighed and rocked back on her heels. "Finished at last. Finished at last." She stuck her fingers in the front pockets of her corduroy slacks, her typical work pants, paired with a thermal top. She preferred the fitted material, because looser clothes had the potential to fall forward when she was working. Not a good thing if she was using her torch. "I think this just might be my most involved project yet."

"You should be very proud, Sami." Jack moved up and put his arm around Tate's shoulders. "It's really something special."

"You've seen it?" Tate asked, putting her hands on her hips. "She never lets me look until it's done."

"Me either," their mother said, hiking a brow.

"I never let anyone see." Sami shrugged. "But Jack's different. He's an artist too."

"He certainly is," Tate crooned, leaning into her husband for a quick kiss.

Fiona couldn't help smiling at the lovebirds. She was so happy for them both, so relieved the high school sweethearts had found their way back to each other. Even if the trip had been a bit rocky.

Her heart gave a little sigh, and she wondered if she'd one day find someone she could love that way. A man who was strong yet tender. Loyal, dependable, and steady as the rain.

When Ronan's face floated to the surface, she went utterly still. Her breath caught in her lungs as shame slapped down the romantic musings.

Why had he come to mind? He was the last man—in *all* the worlds—who should ever enter her starry-eyed fantasies.

She coughed to clear the sudden mass from her throat. Talk about a toxic relationship. She could imagine telling their story.

How did you two meet?

He saved my life.

How romantic!

Then he tried to kill me.

Rubbing her eyes, Fiona told herself she was just strung out from the long and wearisome day. It was no wonder her mind was a muddled mess, switching up the roles of hero and villain where Ronan was concerned.

Then again, compared to Emuirdane, the guy didn't seem half bad.

"Don't even think that way," she muttered to herself, unaware she'd spoken aloud until Sami leaned across the table to peer closely at her. "You okay, Fee? You look a little pale."

"I'm fine." Fiona waved away the concern. "Just tired."

Granddad walked around the table, his finger shaking at her. "I told you not to hook up that trailer by yourself. It's heavier than it looks."

Wondering what she'd done to give herself away, Fiona could do nothing but nod in acquiescence. Good thing she knew how to cook. Because she'd make a terrible spy.

"You're right, Granddad. I took it this morning when I went out but brought it back because it was too cumbersome to pull around the whole island." That much, at least, was true.

"Next time wait for us to get home. Or call someone." He chucked her chin on his way to the stove. "Now, Nadia. How long until we eat?" he asked his daughter, who was even now taking the pot off of the hot burner.

"The chicken fingers are ready. They're in the oven to stay warm." Fiona's mother made a face. "I'm still not sure how they'll taste dipped in the Romesco."

"Like heaven," Sami assured her.

Fiona went to the sink to wash her hands. "I'm sorry I wasn't here in time to make dinner."

"Don't be silly," her mother said. "I love cooking for my girls." She winked at Fiona. "Besides, I think you cooked enough meals while I was gone to earn yourself at least one night off."

"Nope. Too bad, Fee." Sami plopped into a chair at the able. "Your family pass has been revoked."

"Oh, leave her alone." Tate tossed a napkin at Sami's face, then gave a rolling chuckle when Sami jerked her head back so hard her hair fell free.

Again, Fiona tensed. But Sami just laughed.

Swiping a glass of tea, Fiona downed half of it and moved to take a seat. She needed to take a break, warm up by the fire, and try to clear her head. Her family would know something was going on if she didn't calm down. *I'm too edgy, too tense, and . . .*

"Fiona."

"What?" She jumped out of her skin. *Too distracted.*

"Easy," Brit said, but her uncle had his stern lawyer face on. Did he suspect something? How could he?

Her family might have magick, but they weren't psychic.

He sat across from her at the table. "I want to tell you something, and I hope you won't be upset."

He couldn't have surprised her more, since she was the one expecting to get caught. She set her empty glass down and beetled her brows, waiting for him to go on.

"I spoke with Joan Wilson a couple of days ago," he said.

Fiona sat up straight. "The realtor who's handling the property on High Street?" The place she'd wanted for her sweet shop. The dream she'd caught sight of, only to have it blow away. "Is it up for rent again?"

Sami had surprised her on her birthday last fall with the news that the retail space was available, but then they'd become embroiled in mystical quests, and the owner of the building had changed his mind, putting the place up for sale instead.

For years she'd stashed away extra funds from her on-the-side dessert business, saving enough for start-up costs and several months' rent. But she was in no position to purchase the property in its entirety.

"No," Brit said, "it's still on the market."

"Oh." Fiona slumped again. She could actually feel the hope draining away.

"But there's another space that's become available. A building I'd like to buy."

Stunned silence met Brit's announcement. No one else, it seemed, had been told of his plan.

"Why would I be upset about that?" Fiona finally asked.

"Because I was hoping you'd be my first tenant."

Her mouth dropped open.

"I thought you might have your heart set on High Street. You talked about its *character* a lot." His expression was that of a man who didn't quite grasp the vagaries of the female mind when it came to décor.

"Oh. Okay," she muttered, still trying to catch up. "But where?"

"Do you know the Morrison building?"

"The brick one?" Tate asked. "The one with the old clock?"

But Fiona zeroed in on another key point. "The one on Main Street?"

Brit nodded.

"That's got to be ..." she recalled info from the property research she'd done and quickly did the math, "double the price."

"My accountant told me I needed to make a big purchase this year to offset taxes." Brit's smile was filled with affection. "And I can't think of a better investment than you and your shop."

"Yes!" Sami slapped a hand on the table.

Mom nodded enthusiastically. "This is the perfect idea."

Fiona's emotions reared up and made a push for release. Eyes burning, she folded her hands in her lap and tried to remain business-like. "That's a generous offer, Brit. But what if I fail? You could lose a lot of money."

"I don't expect that to happen. You have a well thought-out business plan, a good location, and products—I know from personal experience—that will sell faster than you can make them."

"But ... I know how much it will cost, and I can't even afford to go in half with you."

"I'm not asking for that. You'll pay rent, just like any other tenant."

Joy, fear, and guilt all battled for the upper hand as Fiona struggled to make sense of his proposal. "Maybe you should let an established business have the space. I'm too big a risk for you to—"

Brit raised his hand to stop further objection. "Fee," he said softly. His green eyes, so like her own, held a strength and certainty she wished she could match. "I have complete faith in you."

The emotions Fiona had been keeping in check rose to the surface and threatened to spill over.

If only she had such faith in herself.

But hadn't that always been her problem? Emuirdane might be cruel, but what he'd said to her on the road was the truth.

"If you agree," Brit continued, "and I hope you will, I only ask for one thing."

With a hitch in her voice, she asked, "What's that?"

"One of your special chocolate chip cakes."

A huge knot was in her throat, so she only grinned. It was as if he'd read her mind.

As a little girl, she'd been withdrawn, self-isolated, despite the love and support of her sisters, Brit, and Granddad. Both her parents had died before she was three years old, and though they hadn't chosen to leave, she'd still felt abandoned. To the point that her grandfather had taken her to therapy, a year's worth, with little improvement.

Then came the Christmas that had changed her life forever. Thanks to a big red box with an Easy-Bake oven inside.

Mixing the little packets of powder and water had felt like magick, and to watch them rise—and ooh, the smell! For the first time, she couldn't wait to share something with someone else.

Her sisters had loved the strawberry, and Granddad the vanilla. But Brit had made a special request.

He'd asked her to add chocolate chips to his cake.

Ever since that day, baking had been her haven. Not only did she love to create, but the results made others happy too.

"I can't believe you remember that cake." She laughed through the tears that now ran freely.

"Little Fee." Brit wiped her cheek. "When are you going to start giving yourself more credit?"

And just like that, her conscience became clear. Not only would she lie to the people she loved most in the world, she'd do so with a smile on her face.

If it took deception to protect her family, then so be it. Anything to keep them free of Emuirdane's torment.

She ran her fingers over the front pocket of her pants where she'd stuck the card Ronan had given her. She could see no other way to move forward.

Emuirdane wanted the Ceffyl.

Ronan could summon the Ceffyl.

But only if Fiona agreed to conspire with him.

So, fine. That's what she'd do, walking a thin line to keep her two enemies happy and safeguarding her family in the process.

Tomorrow she'd go to the inn, and this time she'd be the one showing up unannounced. She'd meet with Ronan and find out exactly what he had in mind.

But only after she swung by Main Street and took a peek into what might be her dream come true.

"Uncle Brit." Fiona stuck out her hand, feeling better, feeling stronger than she had all day. "You've got a deal."

7

Fiona stared up at the Morrison building and felt inclined to give herself the proverbial pinch. Never in all of her fantasies—and she'd had many—had she ever imagined opening her shop in such a beautiful and historic place. And, she reminded herself, right on Main Street!

Three classic stories of brick boasted a black wrought iron balcony on the second floor with a white Colonial façade below on ground level. Slowly, she studied the elegant frontage and all its details, especially appreciative of the pineapples across the top, symbols of hospitality and welcome.

It's perfect. She gave in and hugged herself, but restrained from doing a happy dance on the sidewalk. *Just perfect.*

Brit was right. The location was too good an investment opportunity to pass up, and she would have encouraged him to buy it whether she rented the space or not.

"Right down the street from my office," he'd told her this morning with a wink, "so I can satisfy my sweet tooth any time."

Fiona still felt like he was doing her a favor, but knowing he would benefit regardless of her store's performance chased away the last shadows of worry. Leaving room for all the hope she'd stored away for . . . well, as long as she could remember.

"My shop. It's finally happening." And this time she did dance. Just a little. A single discreet hop and jiggle to release some of her pent-up joy.

Hands cupping the window glass, she peered inside at a well-kept interior, formerly a bookshop that had moved to a larger storefront. She could certainly keep some of the built-in shelves, use them to display specialty baking items, but the majority of those freestanding racks would have to go.

She wanted plenty of room for the cute little tables she'd found online. White and whimsical, they'd pair well with most colors, and she definitely wanted a charming atmosphere. A place where people would meet for morning scones with coffee, and stop by after work to pick up brownies for their wives, or custom birthday cakes for the kids.

The wood floors were in great shape, but maybe she could stain them a rich cappuccino color, to set off the lighter accents . . . and there, on the wall! Just the right spot for the piece of art Sami had made for her last year.

Cakes, cookies, pies, divinity—you name the confection and Fiona would likely feature it at some point. In her favorite fantasy, her very own shop. *The Sweetery.*

Her eyes watered, so she spun around to look down the street and allow the breeze to dry any remnants of her happy tears. After a moment, reality and her other reasons for being in town began to creep back in, so she clamped down on the planning and dreaming.

She couldn't get too excited, not just yet. There would be no dreams coming true for her or anyone else in her family, not as long as Emuirdane was still lurking. His vengeance was like a guillotine, just waiting to drop.

The wicked Iele had to go, and she was the only one who'd been given a chance to make that happen.

Feeling twitchy now, she tapped her toes and pictured Ronan's disdainful face. To her great misfortune, she needed his help and couldn't waste another three months searching for the Ceff—for Jewel.

The Legion warrior had proffered a partnership, and Fiona was resolved to do whatever it took to find the horse and put an end to Emuirdane's tyranny. Even if that meant lying to her family.

Even if that meant working with *him*.

Before she gave Ronan her answer, however, she would arm herself with as much information as possible, so she needed to check in with one more person.

She cast her gaze to the opposite corner, to a cream-colored clapboard with forest green trim. She made her way to the crosswalk at Main Street, hurried over, then waited for the signal to cross Cottage Street.

She couldn't stop grinning as she made the short trip, imagining herself popping over like this now and again, bringing coffee and cookies to share with her new retail neighbor.

She stopped before a door with a weathered wooden sign swaying in its chains, proof that the ocean winds were in full force. Pushing her way inside, she heard the tinkle of bells and inhaled a fresh, fruity scent. The candle of the day smelled like some type of berry.

Rows of jarred candles lined the walls and other display racks, spaced in perfect order like tiers of colorful soldiers. In addition to the lovely smell, a different sort of sensation rolled straight through Fiona. Warm, invigorating, and as familiar as her own skin.

She closed her eyes and embraced the awareness. Of *magick*.

Kat stood behind the counter, her sunbeam-hair pulled back in a sleek ponytail. She handed an ivory box to her customer. "Here you go, Annie. I expect I'll see you again when summer rolls around."

"Will you have those strawberry-cream candles again?"

"Of course."

"Then you'd better stock extra for me," Annie said with a laugh. "My twin sisters have a birthday in June. I want plenty for them," she winked, "and myself."

"You got it." Kat tossed a little wave to the woman and waited until the door closed behind her before giving her full attention to Fiona.

"Fee," Kat said, her smile blooming like a spring flower. "I'd hoped you'd drop by." She raised her pale brows and gave Fiona an appraising onceover. "And don't you look like a woman with good news to share."

Fiona lifted her hands and let them flop back down to her sides. "How do you do that? You sure you aren't psychic?"

"Psychic? No." Kat shrugged. "Maybe a bit of an empath." Her gaze dropped to Fiona's jacket pocket. "No luck yet with your own sensitivity?"

With a crooked grin, Fiona retrieved the Blue John fluorite from her coat. "There's no way you sensed this." Kat had helped her choose the yellow and blue striped stone the day she and her sisters first came here for help.

"No. But I did see your hand hover over that pocket when you walked in." Kat's chuckle was smooth as velvet. "If I didn't love my candles so much, I might take a turn at fortune telling."

"You'd make a killing." With a shake of her head, Fiona moved to peruse a nearby shelf, fascinated as always by the many colors, the blend of enticing scents. While the candle store was the business people saw from the streets, the products out front weren't the only ones Kat dealt in.

Behind the storage room and down a short hallway stood a blue door with metallic sun and moon emblems. Beyond the door was where the magick lived. Crystals, wands, grimoires—an array of arcane items and tools for the craft could be found in Kat's back room.

Fiona reached into her pocket and caressed her own crystal again, remembering how the stone had caught her eye. How it had *called* to her.

Since that day, she'd discovered so much about herself, her powers, and her family history. And whenever she needed a respite, a break from dealing with wicked faeries—or extra advice on *how* to deal with them—she'd always find her way here, to Kat's.

Today was no exception, but at least she'd brought some joy to balance the usual talk of Emuirdane and his hold on the Whiteburns.

"I stopped by for a couple of reasons," Fiona said, "and one of them is actually about business." She couldn't repress her grin. "It looks like I'll finally be opening a store of my own."

"Oh, Fee!" Arms flung wide, Kat rushed from behind the counter and wrapped her in a congratulatory hug. "I'm so, so happy for you." She pulled back to ask, "The place on High Street?"

"No. That's where my news gets even better." Taking the other woman's hand, Fiona led her to a window and pointed to the brick building across the intersection.

"The Morrison place?" Kat's eyes bugged. "Are you serious? I didn't even know it was available for rent."

Fiona shook her head. "Up for *sale*. And before you ask, I'm not buying it. Brit is, and he wants me to be his tenant."

"Well." Kat crossed her arms in a ladylike fashion and hiked one brow. "I'm glad to see he's doing something to make up for binding you all those years."

"Kat." Fiona's voice held playful reproach as she reached for a pale purple candle. She took a sniff. "*Hmm.*" She'd found the source of the fruity smell. "That's wonderful."

"It's called Snowberry, and with spring coming I've put these on sale."

"Then I'll take three," Fiona said. "But only if you promise to cut Uncle Brit some slack. He and Granddad only did it to protect us."

"*Pffft.*" Kat waved both hands in a whatever-you-say gesture. As a local witch, she'd always known the Whiteburn family secret. In fact, she'd been aware of the sisters' abilities long before they had.

After Nadia's death—when they'd all still believed she'd actually died—Brit and Granddad had worked a spell to repress the magick

Fiona and her sisters possessed. Granddad had felt strongly that Fiona's mother had died because of her power, that she'd been preparing for something in the days before her death.

He'd never known the full truth but, lost in grief for his daughter, he'd decided not to take any more chances with the mystical world.

Especially with three innocent little girls that were now his to raise.

Brit had been just a teenager then, but he'd agreed, lending his own abilities to help his father work a powerful enchantment. Growing up, Fiona and her sisters had never felt the smallest spark of magick.

They'd only learned of their powers when a goddess sent her messenger to set them on their first quest. Three days to find the key to their happiness, their magick, and their very lives.

This key, it turned out, was their still-very-much-alive mother.

Their mother *had* been expecting trouble just before her death. So when Emuirdane's wife, Hellana, had come to kill her daughters, Nadia was ready.

Their two mighty forces collided, trapping both women in a system of tunnels below the ground. And there they'd been confined, a human witch and an Iele Fae. One sleeping, one waiting.

For twenty years.

Fiona sniffed the berry candle again, letting the sweet smell drive away the memory of her childhood heartbreak. She was here to focus on positive things, on the future she planned to build. No matter what had gone before, she had her mother back in her life, and she intended to make the most of the time they had now.

"I want to hear all about the shop," Kat said, rubbing her hands together. "Now that you have the space nailed down, the real fun can begin. But," she hedged, a knowing twinkle in her eye, "you said business was only one reason you came by, and I suspect I know the second."

"You found something," Fiona said, barely suppressing her excitement.

Kat's satisfied expression said she'd discovered something important. Not only was she knowledgeable of the craft and its related lore, but she also had contacts all over the world.

"I have a friend who owns a bookstore in Savannah. She deals in *rare* finds." Kat wiggled her pale brows. "If you know what I mean."

"Did she find a book about the Jeweled Ceffyl?" Cool skitters of anticipation raced up the back of Fiona's neck.

"Wait one minute." Kat hurried to lock the front door, putting up a sign that stated she'd be back in five minutes. Then she motioned for Fiona to follow her.

Together they passed through the storeroom and into the hall before veering into Kat's office. Unlike the plain and serviceable storage area, this space was decked out with lush décor meant for comfort—rich burgundy chairs, an Ushak rug, and expensive wooden shelves displaying exotic pieces from around the globe.

In the center sat a large shiny desk, as neat and tidy as its owner. Kat unlocked a top drawer and retrieved a small tome, so old and worn, the writing on its cover was illegible. "This is from the early nineteen hundreds." She took a dramatic pause. "It was written in Wales."

Comprehension went off like fireworks. Wales was the country where the Ceffyl originated and where Fiona's grandfather had been born and raised.

"It's titled as a collection of folktales and myths," Kat said, "but it has more information than I've found in any other source."

"Does it line up with my grandfather's story about the Ceffyl?"

"Yes, it's all essentially the same. It mentions Idwal Faol and his attack on the castle, how a boy was trapped outside the gates."

Fiona picked up the tale. "So he prayed to the gods for help, and they sent a white horse, the Jeweled Ceffyl, to grant his wish."

"But what this book details is the origin of the Ceffyl." Kat rubbed reverent fingers over the cover. "Specifically," she slid her gaze to Fiona, "it tells *who* created it."

Those cool skitters were on the back of Fiona's neck again, and she wondered if her "sensitivity" was working after all. Because she had a feeling she knew what Kat was going to say next.

Kat held up the book. "The Dea Matrona."

Fiona closed her eyes when her suspicions were confirmed and slowly loosed a breath through pursed lips. "Of course. It's all connected."

Putting both hands on the desk, she focused on the gleaming mahogany as pieces clicked together in her mind. "The Dea Matrona protects animals and children. I always thought that was why she'd decided to help my sisters and me."

Kat set down the book. "Three little girls whose lives had been altered by a cruel Iele like Hellana."

"But there's more to it than that. The goddess created the Ceffyl, yet she helped us discover our powers when she had to know we were the ones prophesied to find the statue in Faerie."

"If the Ceffyl was supposedly safe there, guarded by the Legion," Kat said, putting a finger to her lips in thought, "then why would the Dea Matrona do anything that would help you bring it here?"

"Exactly my question." Fiona stared at the small black book as if the answer would rise from its yellowed pages. "None of this makes sense."

For a moment, the two women absorbed the implications of the dots they'd connected, then Fiona said, "She must have some reason for wanting the Ceffyl here in the human world."

Kat tilted her head and furrowed her brow. "Then why hasn't she contacted you or sent her messenger? More importantly, the goddess would never want the Ceffyl in the hands of an Iele, so why hasn't she done anything to keep you from giving the horse to Emuirdane?"

A void opened up inside Fiona, but the empty hole quickly filled with a cold and unsettling suspicion. A suspicion centered around one individual.

Ronan.

"Why hasn't the Dea Matrona tried to stop you?" Kat repeated.

Fiona only shrugged as if she had no idea, but a different response flitted through her head.

Maybe she has.

8

Shielding her eyes from the sun, Fiona studied the inn where Ronan was staying. Brick walkways curved through manicured lawns, a fountain gurgled near the entrance, and stone walls arched elegantly over doors and windows.

She followed wide steps inside to the foyer and paused at the reception area. No one manned the desk, so she moved to a nearby hallway to take a peek. Still not a person in sight, only two doors that mirrored each other at the far end. After another quick glance around, she eased her way down the corridor to see if the doors were marked.

The rooms weren't numbered but named with titles like the "Purple Room" or "Morrigan's Suite," the kind of personal touch this type of historical inn preferred. She noted the name of Ronan's room and was overcome by a rush of nervousness.

She double-checked the card he'd given her. Yes. This was the place. The confirmation made her feel short of breath, and her skin seemed to be trying to crawl off of her bones.

Should she be doing this? Was she making a mistake? Not only was she lying to her family, but she was about to engage with a dangerous man. Without any backup.

But wasn't that what he'd planned all along? His ultimatum forced her to deal with him on her own, and she couldn't help wondering why he'd singled her out.

Because I'm the weak one. Emuirdane's words had hit home for her, as if he'd found a sore spot in her psyche, a vulnerable place to apply more pressure.

Well, it wouldn't work, Fiona decided. Maybe she didn't have Tate's take-care-of-business manner, or Sami's ability to shrug off disaster, but she did have strengths of her own.

Even her sisters said the power they all shared came most easily to Fiona. She'd been the first to feel the special hum in her blood, the first to call a white flame to her palm. The first to fully embrace their gift.

In a life riddled with self-doubt, the craft had become a place of comfort. A place of confidence.

She could use a dose of that confidence now, so breathing deeply, she allowed her magick to flow. A bolstering reminder of the power she wielded, the sensation coursed through her like silk lightning.

Before second thoughts could formulate again, she made a fist and gave the door three quick raps.

Seconds crawled by with no answer. She held on to the sense of fortitude, but the time dragged by, taunting her, and the longer she waited the more her skin prickled with sharp, tiny points.

I should have called first. Maybe he's out. After her rush of courage, his absence felt rather anti-climactic, so she stepped back, ready to leave a message at the front desk. But then the door swooshed open, and there he stood.

Ronan's dark hair was damp, his broad chest bare.

And everything in Fiona's mind just flew away.

"Fiona," he said, his voice deep and rich enough to reach down inside of her.

She swallowed once. And again. "Ronan, I came to talk . . ." she stuttered, "I mean, to tell . . ."

Her gaze darted over his shoulder into safe, empty space. "Could you put on a shirt?"

He grunted and mumbled something indiscernible but turned

and went back inside.

Fiona, meanwhile, did her best not to watch him. He'd clearly just gotten out of the shower, but why hadn't he taken ten more seconds to get fully dressed? Why had he come to the door like that?

And why did the sight of him—all those well-defined muscles— make her belly go light in a disturbingly pleasant way?

He's the enemy. Don't forget that. She crossed her arms and cleared her mind of lurid imaginings. Still, her eyes strayed to his lower back, to the rigid strength that dipped and curved nicely to a tight, round—

"To tell me what?" His sharp question wrenched her back to the reason she was here. Which, by the way, was not to ogle his assets.

She stepped inside and closed the door behind her, keeping their possibly volatile discussion private. She made herself remember the terror she'd felt on the bridge in Faerie—the bombs he'd thrown, the crumbling stone, the deadly drop below.

Once she'd stoked her ire and cleared her perspective, she said, "I came to tell you that we will work together," wording her statement carefully, to sound as if she were the one laying down the rules, as if she didn't feel out of control. And completely out of her depths.

If Ronan recognized the pretense, he gave no indication. "Wise decision," was all he said, strolling back toward her while he stretched a black T-shirt down over his stomach.

Fiona blinked. It was no secret that he was a soldier, severely disciplined and in excellent physical shape. But the sight of his corded abs reminded her exactly what she was dealing with. A finely honed weapon. A trained killer.

And possibly an assassin sent by a goddess.

When she thought of it that way, the odds seemed so *not* in her favor. Anxiety spiked, and she tucked her bottom lip between her teeth. Then she reached to trace her fingers over her scar, indulging in two nervous habits at once.

But she stopped just short of touching the scar, the remnant of the wound Ronan had treated when he'd saved her life.

And his generosity hadn't ended there. He'd also helped her family get her to the safety of the Winter Queen's country manor, and later had come back to check on her. Then, upon hearing she'd woken from her poisoned sleep, he'd arranged for a very special gift, a celebration of her recovery.

Standing in his hotel room now, Fiona pictured how the forest had been filled with floating lights, each tree illuminated in pink, blue, green, or gold. The tiny, glowing faeries had been too many to count, creating a vision of fantasy come true.

She and Sami had danced among the sweet little creatures, laughing like two carefree young girls. It was a happy memory and one she called upon often.

Fiona dropped her hand. She stopped biting her lip. Then she released a frustrated huff. She couldn't get a handle on who he really was.

Bombed bridges or faerie parties. Will the real Ronan Gates please stand up?

If she kept weighing the pros and cons of his behavior, she'd make herself crazy, losing her mind before Emuirdane could fulfill any of his sadistic promises.

So okay, she told herself, she'd work with Ronan but remain vigilant, at least until she understood him better. For now, she didn't know if he was actually trying to help her, or conning her out of the Ceffyl's discarded gemstones. Regardless, his offer was the best she would get.

And the only way she would ever see Jewel again.

"So where do we start?" she asked. He seemed to be waiting for her to come farther inside, but she refused to budge from her safe position by the door.

His grim expression told her he noticed. "You can sit down,

Fiona. I'm not going to attack you." He gestured to a Prussian blue sofa, dainty and feminine. She marveled his weight hadn't snapped it in two.

Despite the invitation—or had it been a command?—she remained close to the exit. In case of emergency.

His amber eyes blazed, but at length he sighed and turned his back on her, moving to a set of patio doors. He gazed through the glass panes, past the hedges outside, and to the steel-blue water of the harbor.

Fiona waited.

Ronan didn't speak. He didn't move or give any sign he felt her presence.

After a moment she began to feel foolish, so she relented, walking to the sofa to take a seat.

The second her bottom touched down, he said, "We need to get some things straight."

This time, it was Fiona's turn to use the strategy of silence, prompting him to continue. To explain what he felt they needed to clarify.

"Neither one of us is happy with this arrangement, but we're in a situation that arose from decisions we both made." Ronan shifted his gaze to her, his jaw clenched. "Dealing with each other is the price we have to pay."

He sounded as if he dreaded the prospect of spending time with her as much as she did him. She shouldn't have been surprised, or even mildly annoyed.

Oddly enough, she was both of those things.

"You're the one who's insisting we do this together," she pointed out, threading her fingers and resting them on her knees. "You made the demands. Or rather, you issued the threats."

"No. I warned you I would fulfill my duty and protect the Ceffyl. That's not the same as a threat."

Fiona started to argue that they were exactly the same thing, but she gripped her hands together and bit down on the words. She couldn't explain how losing Jewel would essentially sentence her family to a lifetime of torture and suffering. He'd only want to know everything.

And there was no way she was telling him about Emuirdane.

Ronan would never allow the Ceffyl to end up in the hands of an Iele, a species of Fae who were, by all accounts, far more malicious than the inhabitants of Faerie.

"Fine," she said, exasperation driving her to her feet again. "Let's not get lost in semantics. You say protect, I say threaten. What it comes down to is that we want the same thing and have no choice but to work together. I have the jewels that you need to change the Ceffyl to a statue—"

"And the only way you're going to see the horse again is if I summon her." Ronan moved swiftly, striding in her direction.

Startled, Fiona jumped to the side, putting the coffee table between them. As if the flimsy barrier would do any good. She'd been on the destructive end of Ronan's wrath in Faerie.

And he didn't have to be in arm's reach to commit violence.

His next actions, though, were the opposite of what she expected. He stopped abruptly and held up his hands. He even retreated a step or two, allowing a comfortable space to buffer them.

After raking a hand through his hair, he dropped his arms. "How are we supposed to do this if you can't be within five feet of me?"

Fiona bristled, embarrassed by her own over-reaction. She'd jumped like a rabbit in the brush.

"It might help if you didn't scowl at me all the time." She shrugged, hoping she could pull off Sami's signature move of nonchalance. Where was the bravery she'd conjured before? "And stop jumping like a wolf going for the throat."

Ronan tilted his head, the view of the harbor still behind him. Then he shocked her by kicking up one side of his mouth. "I'll take it under advisement."

Fiona's jaw literally dropped. Was he . . . teasing her? Had he just made a joke? Where was the sullen man who didn't want anything to do with her?

Annoyed by his reversal—more evidence of his quick-change personality—she put her hands on her hips and allowed her pulse to level out again. "Okay. Right. Let's try again from the beginning. When and how do we summon the Ceffyl?"

He held up a hand. "First things first. Before we worry about the horse, we need to take a trip."

"A trip?" Go somewhere alone with him? He couldn't be serious. "I think we've established my lack of trust, so traveling with you is not an option."

He angled his body toward her. "I'm afraid it will have to be." His tone had changed, hardened, becoming that of a man accustomed to giving orders. "That is, if you want to change the Ceffyl back."

Fiona massaged her temples to ward off the stress headache she could feel starting up. "No, no, no. You can't just keep changing the agreement as it fits your needs. You should have told me this yesterday."

"I didn't know then."

She folded her arms and reminded herself of all that was at stake. She should at least find out what he wanted before denying him outright. "So where is it we have to go?"

He paused, considering. "A place you've never been before. A place *I've* never been before."

"Stop being vague. If you expect me to cooperate, I need details. How will we travel?" Fiona held out her hands. "Will I need my passport?"

At that, Ronan gave a sharp laugh and shook his head. "We won't be using standard transportation."

Apprehension began a slow spiral in Fiona's gut. The last time she'd traveled by non-standard means, she'd leapt through a portal with no idea what waited on the other end.

She wasn't eager to relive the experience.

"Just tell me."

"All right." He drew a breath and creased his brow. "I've received orders to report to my superior, to the Legion's highest authority. And I'm to bring you with me."

That was hardly the answer she'd imagined. "But . . . I thought you commanded the Legion."

"In Faerie, yes. But ultimately, I answer to her."

Fiona stilled. The spiral in her belly turned to dread, a sense of impending doom that coursed outward from her center, chilling her entire body. *I was right.*

Ronan wasn't talking about another warrior. He'd said *her.*

The one who'd created the Jeweled Ceffyl. The one who'd made sure Fiona and her sisters discovered their powers. The same one who'd sent Ronan here, to track Fiona down.

All her suspicions crystallized, and as fear swam up to her throat, she took a step back. "You can't be serious."

"Fiona," he said, the commanding tone softening again. "Listen to me."

She retreated until the back of her legs bumped against the bed.

"We must journey to the world of Aurellia."

She didn't want to hear the rest.

But he told her anyway.

"We've been summoned by the goddess."

9

A sense of déjà vu washed over Ronan as he watched Fiona's face turn white, just as it had when he'd surprised her in the stables. She pressed her fingers to her chest, just below her collarbone.

Exactly where the cretid had stung her.

He'd taken note of the gesture when she'd first entered the room, when she'd first closed herself in with him, her would-be murderer. If it were possible, she seemed even more afraid now—of him, the goddess. Probably both.

He waited for that rush of satisfaction, the same sense of righteousness he'd felt before. But it never came. This time, her fear gave him no pleasure, and while he couldn't say why that might be, he didn't allow himself to wonder.

He had a sole purpose, a singular mission, one that didn't involve his personal feelings. After a lifetime of training, years of discipline and routine, there simply was no decision to be made. The Dea Matrona wanted to see Fiona.

Ronan would make it so.

"No." As if Fiona had read his mind, a denial sprang from her lips. "I won't go."

"Fiona—"

"It's not happening." She set her chin in a stubborn expression. "If the goddess needs to tell us something, she can send her messenger."

"She did," Ronan said, moderating his tone, striving for a

midpoint somewhere between persuasive and firm. "Rhiann was here last night. She delivered the missive herself, orders that you and I are to have an audience with the Dea Matrona."

"Then Rhiann can come back again, and we can send our reply through her."

Would he forever be at odds with this woman? "That's not how it works." Ronan didn't want to scare her off, but she needed to understand the gravity of the situation. "Fiona," he added with a hint of warning, "one does not refuse a goddess."

At that she began to pace, rubbing her hands together as she stalked back and forth. Her eyes, though, were downcast, as if she were considering his words.

Finally she paused to ask, "How am I supposed to agree to this? How can I place my life in your hands, or hers, especially knowing what I do now? She's been orchestrating things from the very beginning, so I have to wonder what her true motives are."

"What do you mean?" he asked.

"I mean, why did the Dea Matrona help us find our mother? Because it was the right thing to do?" She advanced on him. "Or were we just pawns? Did she use us to find the Ceffyl and bring it here, away from Faerie? And if so, why would she do that? You keep saying your job is to protect the Ceffyl, so why would she aid us in getting it away from you?"

Good question, Ronan thought, but he could offer no reasonable explanation, and said as much. "I can't guess the motivations of a deity."

She gave a short laugh, more a sound of disbelief. "Right. Like she didn't send you here to trick me, just as you're trying to do now."

"That's not true. I've never had direct contact with her. In Faerie, a council serves as intermediary between the goddess and the Legion."

"I don't believe you. You're just trying to keep me in the dark, at a disadvantage."

"No." Ronan stiffened. "But I can't, and I *won't*, presume to speak for the Dea Matrona."

"How convenient."

He could tell she was slipping away, about to go over the brink of fear and fall straight into panic. Intimidation wouldn't work here. Logic and a sense of security were what she needed, so again, he tempered his voice. "I don't blame you for being concerned."

"Concerned? Try five-seconds from blowing this whole deal out of the water and going straight to my sisters."

Calm and soothing, he reminded himself. "Look. I've told you all I know, and we both have questions." He stepped even closer. "You and I have the same goal. The Ceffyl. I believe the answers we need are in Aurellia."

She crossed her arms, a defensive gesture, but at least she was still here with him. Still arguing. "And I'm just supposed to trust you?"

"Yes. Just as I am trusting you."

"Excuse me?"

"I'm escorting you to a hallowed place—a world that may hold many wonderful and mystical items."

"So?"

Ronan spread his hands. "You're a thief." As the accusation echoed, he clamped his teeth together. But it was too late. The words were already out.

Fiona made a noise in her throat, shooting her arms down by her sides and curling her hands into fists. "I am *not* a thief."

Her cheeks flushed a pretty pink, and she leaned forward as if explaining something to a child. "Listen to me. I'm. Not. Going." She tossed a hand in the air. "Besides, she's a *goddess*, a being who sees and knows everything. What could she possibly want from me?"

"That's what we should find out."

"No. Sorry. This is impossible. I can't just go to . . . to . . ."

"Aurellia."

"I can't just leave this *planet* without telling my family."

Ronan was clinging to patience, but that was the second time she'd thrown her family into the mix. "Let me make myself clear. If you tell them, under any circumstance, our deal is off. Not only will you lose the horse, but I'll still make sure you keep your appointment with the goddess."

He edged closer to where she stood scowling. "I have my orders, Fiona. Don't test me."

Now she retreated, mouth parted slightly.

Ronan had literally backed her into a corner, but she'd left him little choice. All he could do now was repair the damage. "Fiona, you need to understand how—"

Her hands jerked upward, and Ronan froze.

He'd been worried about intimidating her, but she didn't look nervous anymore. She didn't cower, didn't plead or run. Instead she scanned the room, her expression flat as stone, until her gaze landed on the bedside table, on the plate and utensils left over from Ronan's breakfast.

Before he could anticipate, before he could react, the knife rose into the air.

And shot like an arrow at his chest.

Ronan inhaled, tensing for the strike, but the sharp tip stopped an inch from his ribs.

Jewel-green eyes flashing, Fiona held her head high. "Don't test me either, Ronan."

His instincts told him to go on the defensive and dive for his own weapon. To take advantage of the slight opening she'd given him and fight back. That's what years of drilling and preparation would have him do.

But instead he just stood there, studying the woman who'd transitioned before his eyes. She'd gone from meek and uncertain, to bold and unflinching.

This wasn't the first time Ronan had witnessed her two sides, but he didn't feel deceived now as he had in Faerie. Shadows of fear still haunted her eyes, yet she stood her ground, ready to do battle.

No, her aggression didn't anger him, didn't rile his wrath. If anything, he felt a grudging respect.

And something more.

He continued to stare at her, fascinated, until his blood ran thick and hot, pounding through him with a delicious sort of pressure. He recognized the sensation for what it was. Raw, male lust.

And in an instant, his ardor cooled.

His base instincts had steered him off course, and for a split-second, he'd lost sight of his objective. But how was it possible he'd already grown weak? That the woman who'd cost him his pride before was so easily compromising it again?

Ronan locked down his physical response and focused.

Convincing Fiona to accompany him to Aurellia was imperative, and better for all parties if she went of her own free will. With that in mind, he opted for a new strategy.

The two of them were still adversaries at heart, and he'd turned things around on her, asking her to make a show of faith. So it only seemed fair that he do the same.

Careful not to make any defensive moves, Ronan slowly—ever so slowly—grasped the knife's hilt. The sharp tip still pointed toward him, and he could feel the resistance from Fiona's control.

With a flick of her wrist, she could pierce his heart.

But he had a hunch she wouldn't, that she didn't actually want to. Fiona might be a trespasser and a thief, but he didn't believe brutality was in her nature.

Keeping his gaze steady on hers, he gripped more firmly and lowered the knife, being sure to keep the killing end in his direction.

Fiona's brow creased and uncertainty flashed across her face.

Then the fire faded from her eyes, and she lowered her hands, breaking her magick's hold on the blade.

Handle still facing outward, Ronan crossed to her and gently placed the knife in her palm. He wrapped her fingers around the handle, his hand enveloping hers to hold it in place. "I told you I didn't come here to hurt you."

For a moment, they only stared at each other, as if a thread of energy bound them together. Ronan did his best to ignore the warmth of her skin, and how delicate her hand felt in his. "We have to help each other," he said. "Or we both fail."

At last, she released a shaky breath. "How can I take your word after all that happened in Faerie? How?" She shook her head. "You tried to *kill me*."

The harsh reminder severed the thread and broke their brief connection. He released her hand, as well as the knife, and edged away.

"Fiona," he said her name gently, sincerely, "if you believe nothing else about me, know this. My word is my pledge. My word," he said evenly, "is *everything*."

She said nothing, so he took advantage of her silence to provide more evidence. "Think back to the time in Faerie, and you'll recall that I never lied to any of you."

The knife was still in her hand, and she held it out, letting it clatter to the floor. "You just forgot to mention how far you'd go to stop us."

"But I did warn Tate. I told her, in no uncertain terms, that going forward with the quest would bring danger, potentially death. As a Legion warrior, I walk a fine line, but I did what I could to prevent harm without crossing that line. My duties are clear, though sometimes unpleasant."

"But you do them anyway," she said.

"I do." He inclined his head. "I must."

"Okay. You were just doing your job. Let's leave that for now.

But everything you've said only confirms we're on opposing sides." It was her turn to step closer to him. "So what happens when we change Jewel back into the statue? What will you do then?"

"That depends on what you plan to use her for." He wouldn't lie, but chose his words carefully. He was still walking that very thin line. "But if we don't go to Aurellia, we may never find out."

"All of this is so easy for you. You're the one making all the rules, holding the Ceffyl over my head to try and control me."

He couldn't deny the accusation.

"Now you expect me to go to Aurellia and meet the goddess without any assurance that I won't be harmed. Or that I'll even be allowed to return. I can't just disappear, Ronan. Not after what my family's been through."

"I told you I honor my word." Ronan placed his palm to his chest. "I swear, you will be safe by my side."

"What if the goddess sends me away from you? Or if she orders—"

"She won't."

"But how can you be—"

"She won't," he said more sternly. "The Dea Matrona is the great mother, the protector of innocents. She helped you before, don't forget."

"And her reasons for that are still in question."

Ronan didn't push back this time. He had the sense she was having an internal debate, that her resolve was wavering.

She exhaled with a slight groan. "I don't really have a choice, do I?"

"Neither of us does."

"Fine." She stepped around him and headed to the door. "Let's go before I change my mind."

"It's too late in the day," he said, turning to watch her. "Tomorrow. At dawn. Do you know the carriage road bridge near Witch Hole Pond?"

"Of course." She grabbed the doorknob, didn't look back.

"Fiona," he said, "if you don't show up . . ."

The glance she tossed over her shoulder hit him like a slap. "I know. I know. You'll take Jewel away where I'll never see her again." She jerked open the door but held him in her angry gaze. "I'm getting really tired of hearing your threats."

The door slammed behind her and a heavy silence fell.

Ronan spoke to the empty room. "And I'm getting tired of making them."

10

Castle Draviski
The Ielonaar Realm

Hellana reclined against a mound of pillows, silk, satin, velvet—plush and luxurious. Like the rest of her living quarters, her bed was decked out in all shades of blue, the soothing colors of her mother's seaside home.

But the sentimental reminders brought no solace. And despite the grandeur, she was anything but comfortable.

She lifted her arm to inspect the chafed red flesh of her wrist. The manacles she wore were solid steel, heavy and abrasive. They not only restrained her body, but the charmed metal subdued her magic.

The shackles had been commissioned by her husband, who loved her too much to ever let her go. For all of his claims of adoration, he refused to spare her this pain.

Because what he truly relished was her degradation, her humiliation. Through no choice of her own, she was wed to Emuirdane, a formidable king. A heartless monster.

And in a realm populated by Iele Fae, that was saying quite a lot.

A knock sounded on her chamber door, and Hellana reflexively pulled the periwinkle blanket up to her chin. Her body tensed, her stomach revolted, but still she managed a regal tone. "Enter."

She was almost ashamed by how relieved she was when her healer, Veloria, poked her head inside. The woman scanned the bedroom before jerking a nod toward the anti-chamber and sending Hellana a look of query.

Hellana lowered the blankets and released a sigh. "He isn't here." And just as her mistress had done, the other woman relaxed. Emuirdane's absence tended to have that effect.

Veloria's blonde hair, streaked liberally with white, was pulled up in a tight bun. She wore a simple gray frock today, with a white apron fastened around her waist. After hustling inside, she quietly closed the door. "How are you feeling, m'lady?"

The healer crossed to stand by the bed, crinkling her nose when she drew near. "Still sick, I see."

"You mean you *smell*," Hellana said, pointing downward. "The bucket's under the bed."

"I'll replace it." Veloria started to kneel.

"Don't," Hellana snapped, instantly regretting the sharp tone. The healer was one of the few people in the castle who sincerely cared about her welfare. "Please, leave it," she amended with a contrite smile. "I can stand the smell."

Tolerating the putrid stench of her own vomit was a small price to pay if it kept her free of Emuirdane's vile attentions.

Veloria nodded her understanding and set about straightening the bedside table, clearing the soiled handkerchiefs and empty water glass. "I'll get you fresh," she said. "And a bucket of ice so you won't run out in the night."

"Thank you," Hellana said softly, both grateful and shamed by the healer's kindness.

The woman knew why her mistress kept the disgusting mess underneath her bed. She knew and she understood, since the first time she had attended Hellana was after one of Emuirdane's romantic visits.

He had *loved* Hellana to such a degree, a healer had been

summoned.

Bile made a bid for her throat, so she reached for her water, then remembered it was gone. She swallowed and leaned back into her pillows. While she waited, she closed her eyes, trying to envision anything other than her husband's touch, the way his cold black stare devoured her naked body.

And how those cold eyes heated when she couldn't hold back her cries.

She never thought she'd say it, but she was thankful for Emuirdane's obsession with the artifact known as the Jeweled Ceffyl. Only this preoccupation kept him away from her room. Particularly in the last few weeks, when he'd been gone from the kingdom more and more often.

Once, she'd sought to disrupt his search, going so far as to escape Draviski Castle with the enchanted brooch she'd stolen. Its green stone held stores of magick. Magick she'd used to travel to the human world.

Wanting nothing more than revenge against Emuirdane, she'd planned to stop the prophecy he so relied on. Two decades ago, there had been three little girls, the Daughters of Nadia. Three sisters destined to retrieve the Ceffyl from its sacred resting place in Faerie.

So Hellana had devised a terrible scheme, transporting to the mortal realm for a singular purpose.

To slaughter those baby girls.

Her stomach turned over now, but the discomfort she felt was not nausea. The source of this particular distress was something more foreign, and far more disturbing. That uncontrollable and despicable thing called . . . a conscience.

With a moan, she sat up and pressed both hands to her heart as if she could physically rid herself of the guilt that plagued her. Perhaps this new remorse was a result of her wretched condition, or maybe the abuse she suffered at Emuirdane's well-manicured hands.

Whatever the reason, Hellana could not escape her regrets any more than she could escape her bedchamber. All she could do was wait and hope that something—anything—changed her situation.

Every hour she was trapped here increased her misery, and every day brought Emuirdane closer to the Ceffyl.

She pressed a fist to her stomach. She had to find a way to escape again, to get away from Emuirdane.

Before it was too late.

"Here you are, my dove." Veloria chose that moment to return with plenty of fresh linens, a pitcher of ice water and, as promised, a silver bucket of ice. The last was carried by a young footman who wrinkled his nose upon entering the smelly room. He set the ice on the table with undue haste, bowed quickly to Hellana, then fled from the room.

Hellana and Veloria exchanged amused expressions before bursting into laughter.

"Well," the healer said, "I guess we know the bucket under your bed is doing its job."

Another bout of laughter brought tears to their eyes, and Veloria sat casually on the edge of the bed. She took Hellana's hand in her own. "Can I do anything for you, my dove?"

No matter how many times Veloria used the pet name, Hellana was warmed—and stunned—by the freely given affection. She'd received very little tenderness in her lifetime. Hardly any at all since her mother's death.

She didn't deserve such compassion, not after all she'd done. But in her miserable and depressed state, the woman's sympathy was a much-needed balm.

"Thank you, but no," Hellana said. "You do so much already." She rubbed her thumb over the back of Veloria's hand, finding the weathered and freckled skin strangely comforting. "How is your sister recovering?"

Veloria's face fell, a shadow of grief passing quickly across her features. "She is healing, m'lady, and her vision is returning." When she spoke of her sister's *vision*, she didn't refer to her eyesight.

"Ayleen and I aren't young anymore." Veloria's voice was sad, subdued. "The ritual is hard at any time, but particularly at our age."

Hellana squeezed her fingers. Veloria's sister was Emuirdane's oracle and reported the visions she saw in her mind's eye. Visions that were crucial to his pursuit of the Ceffyl.

When Ayleen had failed to see the outcome of the Whiteburn sisters' trip to Faerie and the resulting escape of the horse, Emuirdane had been overcome by his rage. He'd ordered Ayleen's eyes be carved out with a beshouin crystal and the empty sockets cauterized with burning farral herbs.

The ritual resulted in clearer sight and more accurate predictions, but due to the suffering and loss of normal vision, it was a rite oracles normally engaged in of their own free will.

But not in Ayleen's case. "I'm so sorry," Hellana said.

Veloria's bosom lifted and fell with a ragged breath. "It was not of your doing, my dove. And I know—"

The door to the chamber flung open, and Veloria leapt to her feet. She bowed her head and curtsied formally. "My Liege," she said.

Emuirdane filled the doorway.

Hellana's breath froze in her lungs, her blood chilled, and the lush blanket felt suddenly too thin.

Her husband had come to pay a visit.

Emuirdane kept his expression carefully blank, but inside he roiled with disgust. With her glorious blue hair matted and her sleeping shift stained, his beautiful wife was in no condition to receive him properly.

He strode into the room, inhaled through his nose, and shuddered.

"The stench in here is horrid!" He slid his eyes to the old healer assigned to care for Hellana. "My wife, it seems, is rotting in her very bed. If you are no longer fit to attend the queen," he said, smiling in a way that gave another meaning to his next words, "then perhaps I should *retire* you."

The healer, eyes still obediently lowered, clasped her hands and started to speak.

But Hellana beat her to it. "It's not her fault, Emuirdane."

"No? She is your healer, is she not?" The hand he waved at her was jerky with irritation. "Yet you are still bedbound."

The closer he drew to his wife, the stronger the fetor grew, so he glided across the room in search of fresh air. His black boots clomped over the lavish tiles with their intricate pattern as he tried to contain his ire. No expense had been spared on his wife's quarters, yet she still defied him.

And in front of a servant, no less.

He threw open a window and leaned out, so the stiff breeze might draw away the horrific smell. Face still lifted to the wind, he told the healer, "Leave us."

He waited until he heard the old woman's shuffling steps, the opening of the door, before he said curtly, "And wait for me outside." The door closed softly.

Alone with Hellana, he turned his gaze on his wife. "I have been gone from you these past several days. I had hoped to . . . spend time together."

He pretended he didn't see her hands clench on the covers or her neck cord with tension.

"However," he added quickly, "you are clearly unwell."

Her entire body relaxed again.

And fury drummed through his. How dare she show such

disdain, such insolence for her husband. Her *king*!

"I should have that useless old woman beheaded for allowing you to suffer." And for allowing him to suffer.

Hellana's throat bobbed as she swallowed. "Please, Emuirdane. She is helping me, truly. I believe I'm reacting to something in the food, but we haven't discovered what that might be."

Bored, as well as indignant, Emuirdane leaned against the windowsill. "Then I shall have the *cook* beheaded."

"Don't," she said firmly. Then her gaze veered away from him and she softened her demeanor. "I . . . beg of you."

Oh, how it cost her to say those words. A thin smile played about his lips, for he did so love to see her grovel. "Of course, my darling. Anything you wish."

Her blue eyes cut back to him, oceans churning within. She lifted her arms, chains hissing across the fine satin of her bed sheets. "Then I wish for you to remove these."

A long exhalation and, "We've been over this." Emuirdane took two steps in her direction, only to be assaulted again by the stench emanating from her bed. His gorge tried to rise, so he retreated to the window, waving his hand in front of his face.

"You know very well why you must be restrained, Hellana." He leveled a reproachful gaze on his wife. "You ran from me. You took one of my precious stones, and by doing so, diminished my power by half. For twenty years, you left me vulnerable."

He indicated the chains. "As you well know, nothing good comes to those who steal from me. Even the one I cherish most."

"Cherish?" she snapped, but when he nailed her with his gaze, she lowered her eyes and ran a hand through her dingy hair. "I'm ill, Emuirdane. I'm laid low." She rubbed a finger beneath one of her cuffs. "Couldn't you at least—"

"Speaking of those who would take from me." He interrupted her plea for leniency. "I spoke with your father recently."

Now she went stiff and threw her words at him as if each were a killing stone. "I told you never to call him that."

"Fine, fine." He rolled his eyes. "I spoke with *King Malrik*."

"I don't care to hear." She turned her head to stare out another window.

"He has stipulated new demands, in the event I don't deliver the artifact."

With a jolt, Hellana jerked her attention back to him, her mouth trembling. "He doesn't want me back."

"No, darling. I'm afraid he still has no use for you."

She melted into the bed. "Thank the gods." But as soon as she slumped against the pillows, she jerked upright again, her eyes going wide. "The healer, Emuirdane. I need—" Her shoulders jerked and she clamped her lips tightly.

He needed no more encouragement. The sight of his wife on the verge of vomiting propelled him from the room. As instructed the healer was in the hallway, waiting. "She needs you," he spat.

The old woman took a step, but Emuirdane clenched his fingers on her arm and jerked her to him. "This has gone on long enough. Make her better, or I'll take your eyes. Just as I did your sister's."

She bowed her head. "Yes, my Lord."

The sound of retching from inside the bedchamber drove Emuirdane away from the door. He marched down the corridor, enraged over his wife's sickly state. Veloria was reputed to be the best healer in the land, yet still she did no good.

If Hellana didn't improve, and soon, he would do as promised. He would carve the old woman's eyes out himself. Then he would throw her, blind and bleeding, into the kennel, a special treat for his ravenous pets.

Emuirdane had come to see the value of bloodhounds, the same beasts his wife had set loose upon the Whiteburn sisters not so long ago. The hounds were superior trackers. Merciless hunters.

And if those around him continued to disappoint, he would happily put the creatures to use.

11

Fiona woke a full hour before dawn to ensure she wouldn't be late meeting Ronan. She took a quick shower and dressed as quietly as possible, trying not to wake her mother or grandfather.

Shoes in hand, she crept down the stairs, avoiding the squeaky spots in the old wood. Once in the foyer, the breath she'd been holding flowed through her lips, and she silently made her way to the kitchen.

A body filled the doorway of the service hall.

Fiona jumped and barely held back the accompanying squeal.

She did, however, clap a hand to her now-fluttering heart. "Brit," she gasped, "you scared the life out of me."

"I didn't expect anyone to be up." He exhaled loudly, as if he too had been startled. "Why are you sneaking around so early?"

Her heart had slowed but now flipped one more time. She had in fact been sneaking, because her family couldn't find out where she was going today. Or who she was seeing.

Today she had an audience with the Dea Matrona, and the man taking her there was considered an enemy. Fiona still had her own reservations—persistent little warnings that scratched just below the surface—about Ronan, about the goddess. What was their true objective?

Though Ronan had assured her she'd be safe, she still had a cold dark pit inside, one that echoed with the terror she'd locked away.

But, she decided with a sigh, before she worried about that, she had to get past her uncle.

The aroma of French roast rising from the cup in his hand told her he'd had the same idea about coffee. Like her, Brit had a java fixation, just one of the habits she and her uncle shared. They had physical similarities as well, especially with the short pixie-cut Fiona preferred, to the point Tate had started calling them the bookends.

"Did you make a pot?" she asked, hoping to redirect his train of thought.

"Just the cup, sorry. I've got a hearing this morning and wanted to get in early, review my notes at the office first." He continued to block the doorway. "What's your excuse?"

So he wasn't letting her dodge his previous question. "You know, the island is so quiet and calm this time of day. I thought I might—"

"Go looking for the horse?"

The answer he provided was different from the one she'd prepared, but sure. Why not? She'd roll with it. "Early morning is the best time to see movement in the woods."

Brit cast a skeptical eye to the window. "While it's still dark?"

"Dawn," she said quickly. "It lights up the forest floor at a different angle." *I think.*

"I don't know, Fee," he said with a frown. "You never know when or where Emuirdane will pop up."

Tell me about it.

"You shouldn't go out in the dark alone."

His determination was taking hold, and she couldn't afford to be delayed by her well-meaning but stubborn uncle. "I'll give Tate a call. She's less likely to bite my head off than Sami would be if I woke her this early." She conjured up a smile, hoping he bought the act.

Why wouldn't he? She'd didn't make a habit of lying to him. Or anyone else.

Shame was like ash in her mouth, especially when he visibly relaxed and said, "Good. None of us should be going off alone."

Or to a whole other realm. But she couldn't say that, so she swallowed the words along with her guilt. "I'll make my coffee first and give Tate a few more minutes to sleep."

"Jack too," Brit joked.

"I'll give them ten." Fiona didn't wear a watch, but she tapped her wrist. "You'd better go if you want to have time to prepare for that hearing."

"Yeah. I'm gone." He brushed past her in the narrow corridor. "Call Tate," he tossed over his shoulder, heading for the back door and the rear drive where he usually parked.

Fiona rushed to the kitchen and began brewing a single serving, reminding herself she had no choice but to meet Ronan today, as well as the goddess. That taking the risk was her only recourse for reclaiming the Ceffyl and saving her family.

As she waited for her mug to fill, she saw Brit's car exit the driveway and roll toward town.

Another five minutes and she was rolling too.

True to the claim she'd made to her uncle, the island was peaceful this time of day, and she was grateful for the lack of hikers and tourists when she parked in the vicinity of Witch Hole Pond, then got out to walk the rest of the way.

The air held that mystical in-between quality, as it did just before sunrise or sunset. Even in the low light, she could make out the male figure standing near the bridge.

"It's me," Ronan said from the dark, a small light snapping to life in his hand. "The slope is mild, but it's safer to see where we're stepping."

"Why go down?" She gestured farther along the road. "The bridge is over there."

"Not the part we need."

Questions and concerns shot off like rockets in her head as she peered cautiously into the ravine.

He must have read the tension in her pose. "We'll be fine," he said, casting the beam of light toward their route. "But dawn's coming. We should go."

The rising sun seemed to be a crucial factor, leaving her no time for ambivalence. Besides, she'd already come this far, and there really was no turning back. "Lead the way," she told him.

Guided by Ronan's light, they eased over grass and rock, through shrub and tree, until they stood beside the gurgling water flowing beneath Duck Brook Bridge's three arched supports.

Fiona eyed the brook. At least the level was low enough to keep her feet dry if she stepped on the rocks. "Now what?"

"Now we wait for the first light of day," Ronan said.

The early hour was damp and cool, but she enjoyed listening to the titter of wildlife, the wakings and stirrings as animals sensed the rising light. A few minutes passed before she caught the first white shimmer of dawn.

And her stomach fluttered like a bird taking flight. "Ronan," she whispered, drawing his gaze to hers. "Don't forget your promise."

The lines of his face were sketched in shadow, but when he looked at her, the light changed his brown eyes to amber. Without a word, he took Fiona's hand and guided her toward the center tunnel.

Shocked by the casual yet intimate touch, all she could do was hold on.

He glanced back. "Just a few more steps."

Until what? she thought, carefully navigating the slick rocks.

Then Ronan stepped into what looked like a wall of water, an obstruction she'd hadn't seen until his body disturbed it, making ripples as he entered. And though the barrier was clear, she couldn't see him on the other side.

Nothing was visible but his forearm and the hand still holding hers, the fingers that gripped tighter and pulled her through.

On instinct, she took a deep breath, but the liquid wall wasn't water at all. Her vision, however, was filled with glistening particles, countless silver motes floating in the air.

As quickly as they'd entered the portal, they exited. With her hand still clasped in his, Fiona took in the new surroundings. The new world. Before her spread the splendor of Aurellia, home to heavenly creatures.

And the most stunning place she'd ever seen.

Beside her, Ronan chuckled. "Breathe, Fiona."

His prompting made her realize she was holding the air inside her lungs. She smiled—how could she not in such a place of beauty?—and began breathing normally again.

The landscape that greeted her might resemble a forest, but such a simple word didn't do it justice. The tree trunks were so massive they brought redwoods to mind, their bows reaching hundreds of feet toward a cerulean-blue sky.

Great fern-like plants blanketed much of the ground, a thicket of lush undergrowth. Interspersed among the plants were jutting stones, great jagged rocks streaked with a metallic sheen. Everything, it seemed, held a hint of glimmer, the scene made all the more magickal by the soft predawn light.

"Not as terrible as you imagined?" Ronan asked.

"It's beautiful. Amazing." Birdsong, sweet and clear as rain, echoed through the woods. "But Faerie was also beautiful," she said, and by his look, knew she needn't say more.

The most enchanting places could often be the most lethal.

With a jolt, Fiona realized she was still holding his hand. How had it seemed so natural?

She slipped her fingers free and turned away, hoping he hadn't seen the flush in her cheeks.

A blue light suddenly beamed to life, drawing both their gazes. A lantern sat atop an ornate metal rod, illuminating a cobbled pathway into the shadows of the trees. As soon as Fiona moved forward to inspect, another lit up several yards ahead.

Then another and another, until flames of aquamarine cast their glow on the winding footpath that led deeper into the giant timbers and curved up a gradual incline.

"That's our invitation," Ronan said, walking to the trail.

Ronan followed the beacons, and Fiona followed him. A battle waged inside of her, one side caught up in the ethereal glory of Aurellia, the other reminding her to remain vigilant, watchful of both Ronan and the dim terrain surrounding her.

It wasn't until they paused at a gap in the trees that Fiona realized they were high on a mountain. Picturesque and peaceful, a valley spread below, rolling green hills dotted by wildflowers.

They continued upward, stopping only once more by a trickling stream that seemed out of place at such an altitude. The rolling water emitted a sound like singing crystals and fed into a small pond. There, tiny fish darted, glistening in the clear liquid like rubies and gold.

Fiona drew near, captivated by the pond and the deep purple water lilies floating on its surface. She inhaled the sweet scent and grinned back at Ronan. "They smell like honeysuckle."

He nodded but said, "We should move on."

Despite the bewitching forest, she knew she couldn't linger. No amount of stalling would change what lay ahead, her command audience with a deity. "All right," she said with reluctance. "I'm ready."

After a few more twists and turns, they exited the daunting trees only to be greeted by an equally formidable structure. High white walls stretched in both directions, their pristine stones covered by lime-green leaves. The greenery trailed in vines like ivy, but their small round fruits were a shocking pink.

Everything in this world seemed brighter, the colors truer, more vivid with life. She was still cataloging the differences when an arched doorway opened slowly. The vibrant red doors sparkled as they moved, their intricate pattern inlaid with gemstones.

Fiona's shoulders went tense. This was it. What would the goddess say? What would she do?

A woman with hair the color of flames stepped through the gateway and beckoned for them to enter. She seemed familiar, but Fiona couldn't say why.

Once she and Ronan drew closer, he greeted the woman by name. "Hello, Rhiann."

Fiona's steps faltered. "Rhiann," she said. "I didn't recognize you."

"Only because I'm not glowing gold from head to toe." Rhiann gave her a kind smile. "Welcome to Aurellia, Fiona. It is good to see you again. And now that I have the chance, let me tell you how thrilled I was when you and your sisters completed your quest."

Rhiann was the Dea Matrona's messenger, the one who made an appearance at Fiona's birthday to send her and her sisters in search of the mysterious key. "We have you to thank."

Rhiann's expression turned meaningful. "It is not I you should thank."

Fiona nodded her understanding, but the thought of the goddess brought the return of her fears. She clasped her hands together when they began to shake. "I assume you're taking us to the Dea Matrona?" At Rhiann's nod, she said, "What do I do when I meet her? Should I kneel? What should I call her?"

Rhiann waved away her concerns. "No need for such formality. Our lady will know what's in your heart."

Inside, Fiona cringed. The news didn't allay her worries.

Rhiann placed a calming hand on Fiona's shoulder. "Be free of your fears. The goddess bears you no malice."

"If she's not angry with me, then why I am I here?"

Rhiann opened her mouth, her tawny eyes darting between Fiona and Ronan. At last, she said, "You are here to fulfill your purpose."

"What purpose?"

"I can say no more." Lips upturned slightly, Rhiann indicated the open doors. "After you."

As they walked, Ronan leaned close to whisper to Fiona, "Relax."

Easy for him to say. He had served the Dea Matrona his entire life, but Fiona couldn't be sure whose side the goddess was on anymore.

Once inside the walls, her mind went blank as sheer magnificence brought her to a standstill. Marble statues and walkways added elegance to wild and lush foliage. One tiled path led through towering palms to an elaborate garden, and another on the opposite side trailed underneath a long stone arbor that ran rampant with greenery and bright red blossoms.

They turned a corner, and the castle came into view. No, that wasn't quite right. The structure rising from the natural paradise was so graceful, so opulent, the word castle wasn't enough. This, Fiona thought as she started up the white granite steps, this was a *palace*.

The inside was equally impressive, but Fiona found herself less able to enjoy the atmosphere, too distracted by the nerves bouncing around in her stomach again. Every step she took toward the goddess resounded inside, each giving her heart a swift little kick.

Up a sweeping staircase they went and down a wide hallway with open doors at the end. Sunshine filtered in through the opening, telling Fiona they were headed back outside.

Before she exited, she took one last bolstering breath. Then stepped onto a covered balcony.

Morning sun slanted through the surrounding pillars, warming the patterned tiles. Potted plants lined the terrace, framed by a view of the lovely valley far below.

Hands still gripped into a tight ball, Fiona glanced around, searching for an ethereal being. Part of her expected the goddess to glow from within, as Rhiann had done the first time she'd visited.

But what she saw instead was a woman reclining on a sumptuous chaise and, by all accounts, appearing rather . . . *human.* She wore a shimmering gown the color of smoke, basking at her leisure in the brilliant sunbeams.

"My lady, your guests have arrived." Rhiann made the announcement and moved to take up a position near the balustrade, her back to the incredible vista.

The Dea Matrona lifted her head, and Fiona realized her mistake. The lustrous silver hair and luminous eyes could never belong to a mere mortal.

"My lady," Ronan said. "May I present Fiona Whiteburn."

Fiona was focused on the goddess, so Ronan's hand on the small of her back made her give a slight gasp. Even more disconcerting was that he held it there, the heat of his palm reaching through her shirt to brand her skin.

"Fiona." The Dea Matrona beamed at her. "A Daughter of Nadia."

Fiona bowed her head and said, "My lady."

Ronan let his hand fall away, and the spot on her back seemed somehow deprived.

Pay attention, she warned herself. This was not the time to think about Ronan's touch or how it affected her. She stood straight and forced herself to smile, to remain calm. *Keep your eyes open. Keep your guard up.*

Despite both Ronan's and Rhiann's assurances, she couldn't risk becoming complacent.

"You are wise to maintain caution," the goddess said, her iridescent stare still fixed on Fiona. Her eyes were such an unusual combination of colors, yet striking in their beauty, like the inside of a seashell.

And their radiance had just glimpsed inside her mind.

"I don't know your private thoughts," the goddess said, belying her own words by echoing Fiona's thoughts again. "But I am very sensitive to the emotions of mortals."

The Dea Matrona stood in one graceful move and stepped toward Fiona. "And right now, you are all but brimming with suspicion."

Fiona swallowed, her knuckles white from squeezing her hands together. "I mean no offense. My lady," she added quickly.

"I understand. You must be very confused, unsure of who to trust," the goddess said, her voice soothing and warm, like an embrace. "I can tell you that you are among friends, but I know a simple assurance won't suffice, not after all you and your family have been through. So please, feel free to ask your questions of me."

Despite the promise of safety, Fiona's back still ached with stiffness, her hands still wanted to tremble.

Yet the goddess was giving her an opportunity, so she thought back to the beginning, to the night it all began. "You sent Rhiann to our home with information that helped my sisters and me discover our powers. Powers that enabled us to find and rescue our mother."

The Dea Matrona nodded.

"And I've recently discovered that you are the creator of the Jeweled Ceffyl." Fiona licked her lips. "I also suspect you had a hand in creating the heolig, the disc that helped us travel to Faerie."

"I did. Yes." The goddess kept her answer succinct and let Fiona continue.

"You've essentially helped us every step of the way, so I have to believe you wanted us to find the Jeweled Ceffyl." Fiona shot a look to Ronan. "But the Legion soldiers who fought us, who tried to kill us, they answer to you."

"I see. You question my motives."

"I do." Fiona steeled herself. "I'm sorry."

"I intervened on behalf of you and your sisters, but only because other forces had done wrong to your family. Your mother should have remained with you, teaching you. The daughters of Nadia were meant to come into their magick years before." She spread her hands. "When the threat that took your mother reemerged, I simply decided to even the scales."

When the spell trapping Hellana and their mother underground had started to weaken. When Hellana had sent bloodhounds after Fiona and her sisters, another failed attempt to take their lives.

"As to the Legion." The Dea Matrona indicated Ronan. "They are the Ceffyl's army, sworn to defend the artifact. At *any* cost. Some affairs are meant to play themselves out, and I could not interfere in Faerie. I could not have stepped in to help either of you."

Fiona wrinkled her brow. "How do you choose when to intervene?"

"When the balance has been upset by equally intrusive powers. That is all I am allowed." The beads of her gown glistened in the sun as she moved closer. "Even gods must respect prophecy, and contrary to some beliefs, my kind does not, cannot, dictate Fate. It is foolish to try."

"The prophecy has been fulfilled," Fiona said, hearing the strain in her own voice, the frustration. "So why have I been summoned here?"

"Fiona." Ronan's tone held warning.

"I don't mean to be disrespectful, my lady, but I would like to know. What more do you want of me?"

"Not what I want, but what Fate demands." Now the goddess gestured to both Fiona and Ronan. "I've been expecting you for a very long time."

"My lady?" Ronan asked, the bafflement on his face reflecting what Fiona felt as well. Yet he still stood tall, the model of an obedient soldier.

The Dea Matrona laughed and shared a smile with Rhiann. Then she spoke to Ronan. "Of course, it wasn't until you followed

Fiona back to her world that I understood I was expecting the two of you."

The wind kicked up and a cloud blocked the sun.

The Dea Matrona advanced, her gray gown trailing behind. "Long has your arrival here been foretold. Two humans, in this time and place, their destinies merged with that of the Ceffyl."

Fiona waited in silence, the rush of blood singing in her veins.

"These two mortals have been known only as the warrior and the witch." Luminous eyes dancing with mischief, the goddess held out her hands to Fiona and Ronan. "But I believe the description fits."

12

His life had been dictated by Fate.

The air around Ronan felt suddenly charged, as if energy were ramping up, buzzing in his head, until it finally burst in an explosion of light. The balcony on which he stood seemed to tilt, and then right itself again.

He let comprehension sink in, the alteration of all he'd known, all he'd believed.

And once his senses settled down again, he found the Dea Matrona watching him closely. Waiting for his reaction.

But even he wasn't sure how he felt yet. Part of him was relieved by the news, but another, a much larger part—

"This revelation disturbs you, Commander?" The goddess still held him in her hypnotic gaze.

"I . . . it's just that . . ." he fumbled for the right words.

"You have spent your life honoring me with your service," she said. "Like Fiona, you have the right to your questions. Without reprimand."

He bowed his head. "Thank you, my lady." Ronan took his time, formulating his response. Beside him, Fiona appeared shell-shocked. Whatever she'd imagined might happen this day, discovering she was destined to be his partner in yet another prophecy seemed to have left her stunned.

"Your pardon," he said to the goddess. "It's just that . . . if we are these foreseen, the witch and the warrior," he stalled again, then decided to speak plainly, "much of what I've always believed is now cast in doubt. Was my allegiance, my dedication, ever worth anything? If everything was pre-destined . . ."

He couldn't tell her how he'd blamed himself these last months, second-guessing every decision he'd made since first learning that the daughters of Nadia had entered Faerie. That they had finally arrived to seize the Ceffyl.

The sacred artifact they'd stolen in front of his very eyes.

"You question your value," the goddess said, reading his emotions with unsettling accuracy.

"Forgive me, lady, but how can I not?"

"Simply this. Many different scenarios may lead to the same end. Your actions, your choices, are never pre-determined."

"So then, I *did* fail you. My actions, and yes," he slid his eyes to Fiona, "my choices, are what allowed the Ceffyl to be taken."

The Dea Matrona lifted her chin and spoke clearly. "I'll hear no more talk of failure. Have you not served the Legion faithfully these many years and to the best of your ability?"

He stood taller. "I have."

"The Ceffyl is in the mortal world now, perhaps because you chose to let Fiona live. And she triumphed."

He heard Fiona's sharp intake of breath, but he kept his attention on the Dea Matrona. He started to speak, but the goddess held up a finger.

"But if you had not saved her life, she would not be here now, as she has always been meant to be. In your mind you were unsuccessful, but to answer your question," the goddess stepped to him, her liquid gaze intent on his, "you, Ronan Gates, hold *great* value. You followed your training. You fulfilled your sworn oath. But beyond that, you listened to your instincts."

She smiled at him, like a mother to a son. "You listened to your heart."

The relief almost crushed him.

With a whirl of her shiny gown, the goddess turned and strode to the balustrade. She looked out over the mountains, but her voice carried to him. "Strength, intuition, heart. You will need all of these for the task that lies ahead."

She angled her face, addressing Fiona and him. "Both of you have performed well, but now, so much more weighs on your shoulders."

She sighed and dropped her gaze to the sunlit tiles. "Even gods can make mistakes, as I did with the Jeweled Ceffyl. The artifact holds too much power for your kind, and while I saved the life of one child, others were sacrificed. My decision brought destruction, so much pain and grief."

The wind kicked up the silver tips of her hair as she gazed upon them. "But now the time has come, now a chance for redemption."

Ronan's fealty and devotion to the Dea Matrona surged. "My lady, what can we do?"

"I do not know all that will unfold, for the oracles do not tell us everything. And even for the gifted seers, only some visions are clear. More often they are vague. But I can offer you one thing to guide you."

The goddess notched her chin to Rhiann. An unspoken command passed, and the messenger bowed her head before disappearing through another set of doors.

Fiona had remained silent, perhaps giving Ronan his due, his chance to have his own doubts cleared. But now she asked, "Guide us how? What exactly are we meant to do?"

"In truth, I do not know," the goddess said. "My most talented mystic left a gift for you centuries past."

"A gift?" Fiona asked as Ronan eased closer to her. He felt more kinship with the witch than he would have ever thought possible. Fate held them both in its grasp. So it stood to reason, if he'd been absolved of his missteps in Faerie, shouldn't she be forgiven as well?

Rhiann chose that moment to reappear, carrying a wooden cylinder banded with bronze. She offered the object to the goddess.

"Come," the Dea Matrona said to them. "Join me in the sun."

Ronan and Fiona moved as one when the goddess offered the cylinder with both hands. Upon closer inspection, Ronan saw the bands were not simple décor but individual dials. Letters encircled the wooden canister, yet spelled nothing.

He recognized the locking mechanism. "A cryptex?"

"Yes." The Dea Matrona continued to hold out her offering until, finally, Ronan reached out and took it from her upturned palms. "Whatever is inside was intended only for the witch and the warrior."

"It requires a code?" Fiona sent Ronan a side-glance filled with worry.

The goddess nodded. "This is where your destinies align, both of you and the Ceffyl. I put her into human hands long ago, and her future is no longer for me to decide."

In a move that surprised Ronan, the goddess took his free hand in one of hers, and Fiona's with the other. "My faith in you withstands, Commander." She turned to Fiona. "And in you."

Fiona's mouth parted slightly, her surprise evident. Then she bowed her head in respect and acceptance.

"When you begin to doubt yourselves, and you will, you must look to each other for the truth." The Dea Matrona whispered earnestly. "In the end, your hearts want the same thing. And never forget—her wishes demand as much as they grant."

"We will remember," Ronan assured her, and a sliver of doubt pricked at him. He, of course, would never use the Ceffyl for his own gain. He furtively studied Fiona.

He couldn't be certain she'd say the same.

"There is no more I can tell you." The goddess favored them with one last smile. "Providence has called upon you both, and I believe she has chosen well."

With that, her eyes softened, and she released their hands. Her steps were soft and steady as she walked away and entered her palace, leaving them with a new mission, and a mystery to solve.

A presence at Ronan's elbow had him pivoting to face Rhiann. "If you are ready," she said, "I can send you back to the mortal world. Or you are welcome to spend time here. After all, it's not every human who visits one of the heavens before their time."

Ronan was too focused on the wooden container to care much about touring Aurellia. Still, he lifted a brow in Fiona's direction.

She shrugged back at him.

"I will tell you that time moves differently here, as it does in the worlds," Rhiann told them. "If it is a concern."

Fiona jolted. "Then I should go. I'm sorry, Ronan."

"No apology necessary. I understand." He turned to Rhiann. "Thank you. We will return."

"Then hold on to each other." The messenger's lips turned up in a grin full of secrets, as if intimating something more. "Just hold on."

Ronan gripped the cryptex in one hand, Fiona in the other. The same burst of silvery particles filled his sight as it had when he'd traveled through the portal beneath the bridge.

He only had time to blink once, twice, before he and Fiona materialized on the road near Duck Brook Bridge.

But the dawn they'd left behind was now swiftly turning to dusk.

"Oh, no. It's almost dark." A distraught expression on her face, Fiona took a halting step forward. "I've got to go."

"Your family will understand, I'm sure."

"No. They won't. I've been keeping you a secret, remember?" She started off at a brisk pace. "Now I'll have to think of an excuse— more *lies*—about where I've been all day."

Ronan strode beside her, matching her speed. "I'll go with you. Help you explain."

"No," she all but shouted. "They can't know any of this."

"Fiona, everything has changed. We aren't enemies anymore."

She spun around. "Are you so sure?" Pointing to the cylinder in his hand, she said, "We have no idea what's in there or what we're supposed to do next." Her eyes were huge, and a deep, deep green. "I'm sorry, but I can't make any promises until we do."

He wasn't sure what happened, but one minute he was staring down at her, and his hands were on her shoulders, gripping yet tender. Even in the dark he could see the signs of panic. Evidence of the fear that remained.

But why? She had to realize that he and the goddess posed no danger to her or her family.

That's when he recalled what the Dea Matrona had said before. Something about forces that had upset the balance.

And for the goddess to have intervened, to help reset the balance, that could only mean whatever had entered Fiona's life must be supernatural.

She lifted one shoulder, as if to pull away.

But Ronan held on. "What are you afraid of, Fiona? Tell me. I want to help you."

Her voice stretched thin in the waning light, tense with distress. "What we want doesn't always matter." She put her hands on his chest, gave a little push. "Please, Ronan. I need to get home."

She was too upset for Ronan to get any answers now, so he let her go. He watched her rush to her car.

Secrets. Fiona still had secrets that both frightened and enraged her. And whether she liked it or not, her problems were his as well.

As the lights of her car disappeared down the road, Ronan wondered how the two of them would determine the Ceffyl's destiny.

And how Fiona, the green-eyed witch, might affect his.

13

The following morning, Fiona tiptoed through the empty house, peeking into rooms as she went to make sure no one else was home. Avoiding the squeaky spots on the steps, she made her way down then slid around the banister at the bottom.

A phone closet from the early nineteen hundreds remained underneath the stairs, so she opened the door and slid her leather satchel inside. A safe hiding place during the time it took her to grab a cup of coffee.

The satchel contained the grimoire, a book handed down over the years by her ancestors with a wealth of magickal and historical data. She shuddered to think what her family would say if they caught her smuggling it out. Or—now she literally shuddered—discovered who she was taking it to.

On silent feet she made her way, listening for the clatter of movement or hums of conversation. Hearing none, she relaxed marginally and slipped through the service pantry. She moved quickly now, entering the kitchen from the rear. Then she froze.

The slamming car doors she'd heard earlier hadn't been departures, but arrivals. Not only were her mother, grandfather, and uncle still present, but her sisters were here as well.

And judging by their stern expressions, Fiona had just been ambushed.

Her grandfather tapped his cane on the floor. "Leaving early again, are we, Fiona?"

"Uh, yeah. Thought I'd get an early start."

"On what, exactly?" Granddad smiled at her. Like a shark.

"Are we having a family breakfast?" Fiona asked, her voice high-pitched and chipper enough to crack porcelain.

"No." Tate folded her arms, dark eyes sharp and assessing. Despite the early hour, her hair was as sleek and serious as Sami's was wild and free. And while her sisters might vary in their personalities, they seemed united in their current pique.

"You might call it a meeting," Sami said. "One that falls somewhere between intervention and deposition." She plopped into a chair and kicked another out from the table with her foot. "Have a seat, Fee."

"An intervention?" Fiona tried for a laugh, but it sounded brittle and false. "For who?" She veered toward the coffee maker, hoping to pretend distraction until she came up with a plan for escape.

But she stopped short at the sight of Brit's scowl. Leaning against the counter, arms crossed over his chest, he said bluntly, "You told me you'd call Tate yesterday. You never did."

"Oh, that." Her shrug felt pitiful and inadequate. "I changed my mind and decided not to wake her."

"What about later in the day?" Tate lifted her mug in an accusing gesture. "You didn't call me or anyone else, and then you disappeared until nightfall. Brit and I both tried to reach you."

"Then Mom and I got involved." Sami's casual pose belied the anger in her eyes. "We couldn't get you on your phone, Kat hadn't seen you, and no one knew where you were."

"You called Kat?" Rarely had Fiona been chastised by her family, and she bristled at the harsh tones. She'd been apprehensive at first, but the surge of panic was slowly turning to irritation. "You were checking up on me?"

"What else should we have done?" Brit demanded. "We would have stormed your bedroom when you got home last night, but Nadia talked us down. You were out of touch for hours and didn't leave word with anyone. As far as we knew, you were missing. You were *gone*."

The barb hit home and drew a trickle of guilt, but the addition of shame only provoked her further. "I'm so sorry. I didn't realize I had to check my schedule with everyone else. No one ever asks *my* permission for anything. I guess being the baby of the family—"

"Oh, knock it off, Fee." Sami's elbows dropped to the table with a *thunk*. "You've been acting weird lately, sneaking around and keeping secrets. You know how dangerous things are right now. You know we all worry about each other, so blowing us off like that is totally inconsiderate."

Sami jumped to her feet. "Do you have any idea how upset Mom was? We thought Emuirdane had come back. That Hellana had somehow returned and hurt you. Or worse."

"Let's all take it down a notch." Their mother made a calming motion with her hands.

But Fiona was too fired up. She opened her mouth to snap back at her sister, to tell her she had done little else *but* worry about Emuirdane, that she was doing everything she could to find the Ceffyl and get the vicious Iele off of their backs.

But the voice of reason—the voice of their grandfather—cut cleanly through the bickering. "Girls. That's enough." He tapped the cane again to drive the point home.

Sami sat back in her seat. Still, she groused, "Brit's the one who called this meeting."

"Fine, then. I'll be the one to handle it." Lifting his palm to silence his father, Brit stepped forward and faced off with Fiona. "Where did you go yesterday? What did you do?"

"That's two questions at once, Counselor." Fiona ground her teeth together. "And I'm not on the witness stand."

Her uncle pointed a finger at her. "This is serious, Fee. I want to know what's come over you lately. What are you hiding from us?"

"Are you seeing someone?" Tate ventured. "Someone you don't

want us to meet?"

"Am I—" Fiona coughed when her voice broke. But oh, the comment had hit way too close. Feeling suffocated and trapped, she threw up her hands and turned to leave.

Sami's words stopped her in place. "I bet I know what's going on."

Something crashed inside Fiona's chest, as if her heart had broken loose and tumbled down into the dark. She couldn't possibly know. Could she?

"You're looking for the horse. And you're taking it all on yourself because you feel guilty," Sami continued. "But it's time to stop blaming yourself for the horse running away. We don't."

"No, we don't," Tate seconded.

Fiona's shoulders relaxed, and she might have said more, maybe even apologized.

But Sami's hiking boots clunked on the wooden floor as she stood again. "No, we don't blame you for that. But I, for one, resent the hell out of your cloak and dagger routine. This is just not the time for your—"

Fiona whirled on her sister. "For my what, Sami? Not time for me to what?"

"Forget it." Sami waved her off.

Fiona watched her sister walk to the bay window and stare outside, and in those few seconds almost spilled everything. But her mood was agitated and her feelings were hurt, a terrible time to make a confession and field the many questions that would surely follow.

She hadn't slept well in weeks and was overwhelmed. Overburdened. Add to that, she'd been facing conflict on too many fronts—Emuirdane, Ronan, the goddess. And now her family.

All she'd wanted was to fix her mistakes and make things right, but no matter what she did, someone still wanted more. She didn't know why Sami always called her a people pleaser.

Because she seemed to be doing a damn poor job.

"Thanks for the trust, guys." She dragged her heated stare over Brit, Sami, and Tate. "But I think I'll get my coffee in town."

"Fiona." Her mother spoke softly, hands held out. "We're just concerned."

"I know. It's ok, Mom. I'm sorry I made you worry. You too, Granddad." The last thing she wanted was to upset the two of them. "I promise to check in with you more often. But right now . . . I have to get out of here."

Whether a huge rant or a good cry, she was on the verge of an emotional blowout. So before anyone could try and stop her, she hurried back through the service hall and straight to the closet. She snatched the bag with the grimoire and rushed out the back door.

Once safely inside her SUV, she pulled out of the drive and turned on the radio. But the chords of the sad song were more than she could take, and the emotional blowout finally took over.

Hands tight on the wheel and volume turned up, she cried all the way to town.

By the time she got to the library, her face felt like a tomato and she considered standing Ronan up. But she couldn't go back home yet. She wasn't ready to face her family.

Even Ronan had encouraged her to come clean and tell them everything, but he was waiting for her with what might be the final piece of a big confusing puzzle. Together they would open the cryptex and, hopefully, she would know better how to proceed.

She approached the library with its dignified but plain red brick exterior, then entered the gallery and a wash of sunshine. Yellow rays angled down from a domed skylight high above, lending a sheen to parquet floors and elegant woodwork.

Built in the early part of the last century, the building boasted two levels of bookshelves, seating areas, and workstations, backed by antique wainscoting in deep, rich oak. Dual staircases winged up on both sides, so she followed the one on her right to the top level.

She strolled between the stacks and searched the back corners, finding Ronan at one of the secluded tables she'd suggested, a navy-blue peacoat hanging on the back of his chair.

Arms propped on the table and head bowed, Ronan stared down at an open book. Then he looked up with those golden-brown eyes, and a slow, easy grin spread over his face.

Everything inside her went warm and soft.

Until his mouth turned down and he stood abruptly. "You've been crying." In one move, he came around the table and shocked her by gingerly skimming his fingers down her cheek. His tenderness, his concern, soothed emotions she hadn't realized were still so raw.

And for a moment—just a moment—there was nothing in her world but him.

"Come and sit," he said, breaking the spell. He pulled out a chair, pushed her into it, and sat beside her. "Tell me what's wrong."

She thought she'd cried out every tear in her body, but a stubborn few still remained. She blinked away the burn and shook her head. "It's nothing," she said, but a sigh escaped. "It's everything."

When he started to speak, she cut him off. "Ronan, thank you, but the only thing I need right now is to open the cryptex. Can we do that? Just figure it out and see what's inside?"

He nodded. "We can do that." His deep voice held an edge of softness that hummed through her blood like whiskey and honey. Sweet and intoxicating all at once. And when his mouth quirked in a playful half-grin, her heart gave one hard kick in reply.

His brown leather messenger bag looked like something a swashbuckling archaeologist would carry. As he unfastened the buckles, she studied him from below her lashes.

Handsome and strong, of that there was no doubt, but the time she'd spent with him had revealed more of his character. She'd already known he was wily and relentless, but the goddess had imparted a new perspective.

The Dea Matrona had offered him praise, had looked upon him with fondness. She'd commended him not only for fulfilling his duty, but for doing so with honor, intelligence, and compassion. The same compassion that had driven him to save Fiona's life.

She was still admiring his sculpted jawline and full, firm lips when he twisted back around in the chair. She locked her eyes onto the wooden container he held, pretending that's where they'd been all along.

He set the cylinder on the table with care. "Six letters. That's the only clue we've got."

"Which words have you tried so far?"

He pulled his head back in surprise. "I didn't attempt to open the box. Not without you." He lowered his brow, his expression sincere. "You're my partner in truth now, confirmed by the goddess herself."

Whoa. That sounded a little too . . . serious.

So she only bobbed her head in response and picked up the cryptex. The brass dials felt smooth beneath her fingers, but for the letters etched in an old-world fashion.

"Go ahead," he urged. "Give it a try. Just don't force it," he amended quickly when she took the cryptex in both hands. "There may be a failsafe mechanism in these, vinegar or another kind of acidic liquid that destroys the paper inside if you don't unlock it properly."

"Okay," she said a little breathlessly. "No turning unless the lock is disengaged." Forcing her thoughts back to important matters, she asked herself which words might apply to their situation. She went with her first instinct and rotated the dials one by one.

"Magick," Ronan read aloud when she was done. "Good one. Did you feel anything? A shift or click?"

"No." Fiona slumped her shoulders and offered the cylinder to him.

"Why don't you hold on to it?" he said. "You're touch is more ..."

"Delicate? Gentle? Graceful?" she teased.

"I'd say yes to all three." He held his hand up next to hers, the kind of hand that could easily heft a sword. And probably did quite often.

Again she felt a thump in her chest.

Fiona blew out through her lips as through a straw and focused on the small letters once again. "Let's see. Goddess and Matrona are too long. Both have seven letters."

"Try Faerie," he said. " I don't know when this cryptex was made or what the oracle saw before she created it, but it's worth a try. The Ceffyl was in my world for centuries."

Pulling her lips between her teeth, Fiona concentrated and spelled out Faerie. Still a no-go. "Any other ideas?"

Between them they rattled off several six-letter words, but none of their ideas unlocked the box. "Maybe we're making this too hard," Ronan said.

"It *is* hard. The number of letters is all we have to go on." They'd both searched the outside of the cylinder for any hidden symbols or inscriptions.

"Then let's go back to yesterday." He raked a hand through his dark brown hair. "When you first realized this was a cryptex and only one word would open it, what popped into your head?"

She lifted a shoulder. "The word won't fit."

"Just tell me what it was."

Fiona met his gaze. "Jewel," she said. "The first word I thought of was jewel, but that's just the name I gave the horse. And like I told you, it doesn't fit."

Ronan regarded her for several seconds, then he glanced at the cryptex. "Six letters." He narrowed his eyes, tilted his head. "Jewel is only five letters," he said at last.

"That's what I've been saying."

She'd set the wooden container on top of the table, but Ronan picked it up and placed it in her hand again. "Five letters," he said. "In English."

"What?" But as soon as she spoke, Fiona wanted to slap her forehead. "Of course. What were we thinking?" She sat up straighter. "How do you say jewel in Welsh?"

Ronan nodded slowly and smiled. "*Dlysau.*"

Her fingers shook, so she set the cryptex down, wiped her palms on her thighs, and took a deep breath. "I know this is right. It has to be. Because all of a sudden I'm nervous."

She picked up the box again, sliding each dial into place as, letter by letter, Ronan spelled out the word.

They both heard the soft *click*.

"We did it," Fiona whispered.

"Aye, that we did."

Giddy with both relief and joy, she rotated the tube and slid the center of the cryptex out. The smooth wooden tube was hollow inside, except for a small roll of beige parchment.

"Vellum is my guess." Ronan held out his palm. "May I?"

"Of course. Partners, right?" She laughed and placed the tiny scroll in his hand.

After scanning the first few lines, he nodded. "As I suspected. It's written in Welsh. Will you write as I translate?"

Fiona reached past him to grab a pad of paper on the other side of Ronan. When she leaned, she pushed into his chest.

She heard his intake of breath and went completely still.

One strong arm encircled her. He held her close, using his free hand to brush at her bangs.

"Ronan," she said, her heart suddenly feeling three times too large for her body. She leaned into his heat and dropped her hand to his thigh. His muscles tensed beneath her palm.

"I can't stop thinking about you." His thumb brushed her bottom lip. "Can't get your eyes out of my head. Such a brilliant green like the hills of Vidya's Rise."

Fiona didn't know who this Vidya was. And she didn't care. She just wanted Ronan to keep talking to her, with that touch of brogue that had slipped into his voice.

He lowered his head, and her pulse lurched.

"Tell me to stop," he whispered against her lips. "Tell me . . . if it's what you want."

She lifted her mouth to his, and trembled from the welcoming warmth. He started out slow, savoring each glide of skin on skin, then angled his face to take the kiss deeper.

Somewhere inside Fiona, a warning clanged out. A warning she ignored. Pressing closer, she let out a small whimper.

And Ronan's answering moan sounded from deep within his chest. A sound like pain as he broke them apart.

Dazed and bewildered, she put a finger to her sensitive lips. "I didn't tell you to stop."

14

Ronan let Fiona slip from his embrace, her taste still on his tongue and a brand on his chest where her petite body had molded so perfectly. "I shouldn't have done that. I'm sorry."

She blinked and lowered her hand from her mouth. Watching her touch her lip, as if in wonder, had almost made him take her mouth again, even if against his better judgment.

"Ronan," she said, humor in her voice, "of all the things you could have been sorry for, you apologize for kissing me?"

"It's been a challenging week. You've been crying." He opened his palm and looked at the scroll, feeling as if he'd betrayed some higher trust. "I shouldn't have taken advantage of you when your guard was down."

"Oh." She lowered her eyes, folded her hands in her lap. "In that case, you're right."

Remorse curled like a fist in his gut.

And then blew apart when Fiona laughed.

"I'm kidding," she told him, punching him lightly on the thigh. "I know you're the right-hand man of a goddess," she grinned like a hoyden, "but you really need to lighten up."

The playfulness dancing in the green of her eyes allowed the breath straining his ribs to finally release. "Lighten up." He traced the curve of her chin. "Duly noted."

She seemed fine, not upset in the least, but he still felt the need to curb his behavior. He still held certain impressions of Fiona.

In truth, she was powerful, and as brave as any he'd ever known. But when he looked at her, he couldn't help but think . . . Fragile. Sweet. Vulnerable.

Just as the first time he'd seen her in the Ruins of Morogost. In that treacherous and broken-down city of old, their stares had collided. And something had woken inside of Ronan. A thing he'd never thought could exist, not inside his battle-scarred heart.

"Well then."

Fiona's words jarred him back to present day.

She had the pad of paper in front of her and a pen in her hand. "How about that translation?"

"Right," he said and cleared his throat. He unfurled the scroll and began reading, reminding himself he still had a mission to complete and was still in service to the goddess.

"I'll just lay out the basics." He scanned the lines all the way through. "It's a potion."

She'd been tapping on the pad but paused with the pen in the air. "What kind of potion?"

"To change the horse back into a figurine."

Her silence drew his attention, and he found her with a crestfallen look on her face. "You're disappointed?"

Her head moved, but he couldn't say if it was a positive or negative response. "I . . . no. I guess not."

"This states that the Jeweled Ceffyl can only travel between worlds in the inanimate form." He put his hand over hers. "Not so different than what we already believed."

"No. It's no different at all." She jerked her chin toward the scroll. "Does it tell us what to do with her once she's turned back?"

"No." Her despondency seeped into him, and he understood. "So you and I still have opposing goals."

"That depends." Her eyes no longer danced but had fallen flat. "Do you plan to take her back to Faerie?"

"Unless I receive another directive."

"Then it appears we are back where we started." She angled her body away from him, putting the pen to paper. "Go ahead. I need to hear it all."

The connection they'd shared had been far too brief, and already he missed the companionship. Falling back into the role of the prophesied warrior, he relayed the specifics. Business-like. Goal-oriented. Offering no personal viewpoint.

But inside he battled with himself and hoped their path became clear, that their intentions aligned.

"There are some poetic verses here," he explained. "They mention heart and strength, that both will be needed to accomplish the task at hand. Similar to the Dea Matrona's advice."

"What else?" she asked, short and to the point, revealing little emotion.

"Fiona." He reached for her hand, but she pulled away.

She looked down at the pad. "What else?"

Ronan perused the ingredients. "I think we can find most of these quite easily, though you'd be the authority there."

She raised her head. "Read them to me."

"Abramelin oil, graveyard dirt, and a corduroy wrap."

"Hmph," she smiled, as if enjoying a private joke. "I can cut up some of Sami's pants."

"What?"

"Never mind." Though her smile had faltered, she held his gaze. She began to speak, paused, and then, "The ribs in corduroy increase magick's vibration. It's a suitable material for spells that require a quick alteration."

Grateful she was engaging with him again, Ronan sat back in his chair and tried to appear casual. He hoped to put her more at ease. "In all my training of the craft, I've not employed fabrics." He raised a brow. "Ribs, you say?"

That drew a chuckle from Fiona. "I'm not making this stuff up."

"Then explain to me what," he eyed the scroll again, "Abramelin oil is." He'd heard of the substance but found he enjoyed listening as Fiona shared her knowledge of magick with him. For her, he knew, the craft lived inside the heart.

And he wanted as much of that part of her as he could get.

"Abramelin is a sacred oil of Jewish heritage. Legend holds that Abramelin the Mage recorded it in his grimoire. The formula is said to hold great power when used ritualistically." She cocked her head, a glint in her eyes again. "Do I need to explain graveyard dirt as well?"

He took the teasing easily. "Seeing as how the Fae are immortal and turn to pixie dust when they die, we don't have many graveyards."

Narrow-eyed yet grinning, she said, "They turn to pixie dust? Is that a fact?"

He only winked in answer. "Now the last part is interesting. Looks like we need the blood of a Legionnaire." He glanced up at her. "I feel so used."

"I'll be gentle," she said. "Is that all?"

"No, and I don't recognize the last." He studied the last line. "We also need blood from the line of Rhydderch. The name is of Welsh origin, but I can't tell you more than that."

"Wait." She turned to her satchel and retrieved a large book, the ancient cover dyed a deep forest green. "My family's grimoire. It passed to my sisters and me when we came into our powers."

She started flipping the large pages, her fingers gentle with the old and fragile material. "I've seen that name. Here." She stopped and scooted closer to Ronan, bringing the book with her.

He noted the fresh clear ink. "Looks like a recent entry."

"It is. My mother still adds to her section, and since we found out about the prophecy, she's researched the Ceffyl and its stories." Fiona shrugged. "We all have."

Ronan read the passage for himself. "The original child?" he asked with no small amount of surprise. "The child caught beyond the castle gates. His surname was Rhydderch."

"Makes sense." Fiona shifted to face him. "Now all we have to do is find someone with that name and ensure they are a true descendant."

"And politely ask if we can draw some of their blood?"

Fiona closed the book and stood. "Whatever it takes."

"Where are we going?" he asked, standing with her. "To a computer? Search for the name?"

"Yes, but first, some breakfast and caffeine." She packed up the grimoire and hung the satchel on her shoulder, then paused to stare at him. "Come on," she said, her tone gentle as she offered a truce. "Let me buy you a coffee."

How strange was it, Ronan wondered, that he and Fiona could shift so quickly from deciphering a secret code from the gods to lessons on the difference between a cappuccino and a flat white? For the first time, their discussions had held no real purpose—no talk of magick, horses, or jewels.

And for the first time he could recall, he'd put aside his driving need for discipline and self-control, having two fried eggs, ham, and buttered toast. Then a waffle drenched in peaches and juice for no other reason than sheer enjoyment.

Fiona sat across from him at a small round table, and if the contented drowsy look on her face was any indication, she'd been in need of a respite as well. As if sensing his observation, she pulled her attention from the street outside the cafe and settled those brilliant green eyes on him. "Thank you," was all she said.

"For what?"

"For this. A companionable and carefree meal." She folded her napkin and set it next to her plate. "For the break I apparently needed, because I find I'm feeling much better, more centered."

Ronan's impulse was to take her hand across the table, but he locked it down. "You're welcome." He sat back, a hand to his stomach. "I fear I enjoyed the meal too much."

She tilted her head and gave him a half-grin. "I think you can handle the calories."

"Perhaps." He looked out at the sky, a mild day with few clouds. "We could extend the break a bit more." He caught her questioning gaze. "Take a walk. To burn off the calories, of course."

"Or," she said, rising from her seat, "we could walk back to the library as planned."

With a groan, Ronan tossed his napkin down and stood as well. "Back to the grind already? You're quite the taskmaster. I could put you to work with the Legion."

"Ha. You're funny."

He pushed the glass door open before she could get to it. "What's funny?"

"I don't recall seeing any female soldiers in your ranks," she said with a smirk. "I guess feminism and political correctness haven't found their way to Faerie yet."

"The Winter Court has a queen, if you'll recall. I'm thinking she's in no need of liberation."

Fiona laughed at that and started down the sidewalk. "Very true." She wore a light jacket the color of cream and slipped her hands into the pockets as they walked. "Speaking of the Legion, how exactly does one join up? Do they send recruiters to the human world or . . .?"

"Hmm?" It took Ronan a moment to zero in on her question, having been distracted by her sweet scent he'd caught on the wind. She smelled of the meadow, his Fiona, of spring rain and blooming roses.

And when had he begun thinking of her that way? As *his*?

"Recruiters?" he repeated, reining in his train of thought. "Of a sort. Those who return to the human world and start families often send their sons back for training."

"That must be hard on the parents." She tilted her face up toward him. "Was your father in the Legion? Did he send you?"

Ronan nodded.

"How old were you?"

Twelve. That was the answer, but what he told her was, "Old enough." He caught her distraught expression and smiled to ease her concern. "I missed my parents, of course, but I had been raised knowing I would one day have the opportunity."

"So it's a choice?" She seemed somewhat mollified.

"Yes. And there is no better education. Not simply the military strategy and sorcery, but regular schooling as well." He sent her a smug look. "Some of my teachers were Oxford scholars."

"Get out."

Ronan stopped in the street and quickly scrutinized the vicinity. "Get out of what?"

After a moment of stunned silence, she burst out laughing. "You don't know that one?"

He shook his head, then, "Ah. It's an expression."

"Yes. What one might say when they hear news they didn't expect." She continued to grin and they walked on. "So how long does one usually serve? In the Legion?"

"At least to the age of thirty. Some stay longer, some return to the mortal world." He would have elaborated, but they passed a man walking a Golden Retriever. The dog steered straight for Ronan and let out a friendly "Wuff."

"Hey, boy." He started to pet the animal but reminded himself there were stricter rules here than in Faerie. "Do you mind?" he asked the owner.

"No. No. He seems to like you."

Ronan crouched and rubbed behind the dog's ears. "There's a good boy. A fine boy."

Fiona stood by and watched without comment.

Returning to a full stand, Ronan patted the dog on its side, then let him and the man go on their way.

"You're a dog lover," Fiona observed.

"Animals in general. Gentle, unbiased creatures." He hooked his arm through hers without thinking, but she didn't shy away or withdraw.

"So what about you?" She stared straight ahead. "When are you going back to the human world? For good, I mean."

The direct query sent a cold shiver through Ronan. Suddenly uncomfortable with the topic, he hedged and gave a vague answer. "No time soon."

"Are you thirty yet? Sorry," she added quickly. "I'm prying."

Oddly, he didn't mind. In fact, he would share his life story with her if they had the time. But the truth was— "I won't be returning," he said, rushing the words before he could change his mind.

Fiona Whiteburn stirred something in him. He felt a special bond with her, a link that belonged only to them, and had nothing to do with her prophecy or his fate. For that reason, he would be honest with her.

She stopped again, just as they stepped into a crosswalk. He took her hand and led the rest of the way before they were run down by a car. They moved to stand under a pine still green with needles, on the edge of Agamont Park. The slope of grass had yet to recover from winter, and beyond the seawall, dark water churned.

They needed to hurry. A storm was brewing.

"What do you mean?" she asked him. "Why won't you go home?"

A brisk breeze stung his cheeks. "I'm the commander of the Legion, Fiona. I accepted the position knowing full well what it meant. I won't forfeit my post. I won't break my oath. Not until my services are no longer required, or I am too old to lead."

"You'll give up your whole life?" An emotion he couldn't name glittered in her eyes. "That hardly seems fair."

"It's the choice I made."

"I see," she murmured.

Though he didn't think she did.

Confusion tightened the graceful line of her neck, the sweet curve of her cheeks. "You're giving up so much."

"I never saw it that way." *Until I met you.*

She shivered in a chill that seemed to be deepening minute by minute, and this time he listened to his instincts. He wrapped her in his arms. "I'm here now, Fiona. I'm here with you." He cupped her chin. "I'm here *for* you. You only have to let me in, and I'll stand with you against those who would do you harm."

She tensed against him. "Ronan—"

"Let me in," he said gruffly. "What are the forces the Dea Matrona mentioned? Who or what has upset the balance of your life?"

"I . . . it's not my place." She avoided looking at him as she searched for what to say. Then she steeled herself. He could almost feel the wall being erected between them. "The goddess didn't tell you everything, Ronan. I believe she held some things back."

"Why would she?"

"I don't know. Maybe she feared telling you too much would affect your actions. Change your behaviors." Fiona curled her fingers into his coat. "Please, let's just go back to talking about us, just us. Our lives. Talking the way two normal people might if they'd just met in a cafe."

"But we aren't normal people. We've been given great gifts, and with those gifts, great responsibility." He kissed her mouth, slowly, sweetly, then spoke in a soft voice as he shielded her from the biting wind. "You can trust in me. Take me home to your family. Now. Tell them everything. I can see how it's hurting you to deceive them."

She shook her head. "I can't yet. I'm not ready."

"Why not? This makes no sense."

Eyes wide, she started biting her bottom lip. Why did she shut down every time he pushed her on this matter? What was she hiding?

"That's it then," he finished his thought aloud.

"What's it? What?" She clung to him. "Ronan, let's just—"

"You're not afraid of what your family will find out." He caught the flash of panic that crossed her face and knew he was right. "But what *I* will."

A great gust of air shoved against his back, and only then did he notice the quality of the air—thick, scented with sulfur, and tinged a sickly green.

He spun around but kept one protective arm flung across Fiona. "Not a storm," he said more to himself than her.

"Oh, no," she whispered. "Ronan, you have to go."

"This is Fae magick." He scanned the park, still busy with visitors despite the cool weather. "What's here? Why has it come?"

"Ronan." She dug her fingers into his arm and forced him to look at her.

Lightning split the sky as the clouds went black. "Fiona, these people are in danger."

"No. They aren't." Terror ran wild behind her eyes as she looked over his shoulder and trembled. "But we are."

15

Ronan pulled the seelion from his leather pack and tossed the bag aside. Fog rolled in from the sea—too thick and too green to be natural—and all but obscured the park and other people around him.

He glanced over his shoulder to Fiona. "Stay close to me."

"Ronan, please," she said, edging to his front to face him. "You have to trust me on this. Go now."

"You think I would leave you alone? To deal with a Fae by yourself?" He continued to check the surroundings as he spoke. "I don't know why they've come, but I will not—"

"I do," she said quickly, taking his face in her hands. Lightning flared and cracked like gunshot. She flinched, stepping back to scan the area before her stare met Ronan's again. "He's here for me. So please, go. Let me handle this."

Realization was a blow to the gut, and Ronan's body went rigid from top to bottom. This is what she'd been hiding. But why? What dealings could she have with one of their kind? "Who is here for you?"

The clouds above boiled a dark, greenish black. He clenched the blade in his hand. "By the gods, Fiona, what have you done?"

"Not by the gods." An angry male voice reverberated through the tainted air.

Ronan shoved Fiona behind him again and faced the fog where it peeled apart, and a figure emerged. For a moment, he didn't understand. The man was obviously Fae—tall, lean-faced, and bearing the refined attractiveness his kind all shared.

But rarely had he seen a Fae so dark, eyes and hair black as a raven's. Then the man bared two long, sharp fangs.

"Iele," Ronan said, his voice raspy with a blend of horror and rage. A terrible shock raced through him as he tried to understand. How did Fiona know this creature?

He felt her move forward and attempt to stand in front of him again. "Stay back!" he shouted, lunging forward to meet the Iele midway.

He hadn't expected such a threat, not here in the human world. His seelion was crafted from Vellenium, a lethal metal to the Fae beings of Faerie.

But it took gold to kill this monster.

And Ronan had none.

"You will not touch her," he ground out through clenched teeth. Blade raised, he kept himself between the Iele and Fiona.

"You've the right of that, Legion bastard." The Fae approached, his long black coat billowing in the fierce storm he'd created. A jagged shaft of lightning struck the ground between Ronan's feet. "It's not the woman I have come for."

"Emuirdane! Don't!" Arcing out, Fiona kept herself from Ronan's reach and rushed forward. "You can't hurt him!"

"I warned you to stay away from the warrior." The man released a blast of power and sent Fiona flying. "Now your betrayal will cost his life!"

The Iele flicked his hand, but Ronan read his body language and anticipated the attack. He leapt to the side, the intense heat of green lightning flashing past him.

"We need him, Emuirdane." Fiona was back on her feet, yelling against the rising gale. The Iele was using his winds to hold her back.

Ronan had no time to make sense of what she was trying to tell this Iele, this *Emuirdane*. He was too busy watching the Fae as he circled, preparing for his next strike.

This time when the lightning sprang free, Ronan ducked, barely avoiding the slice of energy aimed at his head. The Iele was holding true to his threat.

He meant to end Ronan's life.

With no other choice but to go on the offensive, Ronan surged forward and rolled to the ground, escaping the strike he'd expected.

Fiona screamed his name, but he kept his eyes, his focus, forward on the immortal beast who was trying to kill him.

The wind roared, drowning out her words. He thought he heard her say "Ceffyl."

In a move he'd practiced—a move he'd *instructed*—a million times or more, Ronan feinted left then pivoted to the right and came up just behind his opponent.

One quick jab and he buried one end of the s-shaped seelion in Emuirdane's side, then ripped it back out, doing as much damage as possible.

The Iele bent forward with an "Oof!"

Ronan raised the blade high. He might not have gold, but he'd just see if the bastard could survive without his head.

He swung downward.

Emuirdane dropped to the ground and the sharp edge whistled by, less than an inch from his neck.

But it was all the advantage he needed. Still lying on his back, the Iele threw his hand up and discharged his magick. Straight up. And into Ronan's shoulder.

Ronan roared when what felt like fire ate into his body, devouring flesh, sinew, and bone. The agonizing burn staggered him, took his breath, and blinded his sight. Disoriented, he lost his balance. Then the ground slammed into his face.

"Fiona." He tried to speak, to tell her to flee. But he couldn't see her. Didn't know where she was.

Nausea cramped his stomach as the searing pain continued to spread, crawling through his body like poison. A toxin he could feel doing its damage. Destroying his body.

Something touched his chest. A hand? Two? Had Emuirdane come to deliver the final blow?

"You can't! You can't!"

Fiona. No. He could think the words. He could long to warn her. But Ronan was beyond speech. Blackness came like the tide, washing over him, covering him up. Only to recede again.

"I need him to find the Ceffyl," Fiona said, her voice floating above him. "He's the only one who can summon the horse. I told you I wouldn't betray you. Please, please."

A deeper voice responded with a tone that was clipped and steely with wrath.

But the abyss leapt up and swallowed Ronan whole.

The next time he surfaced, he heard Fiona's distraught voice. "Tate! I need you to come get me!" A sob. "Agamont Park. Hurry, hurry!"

A gentle hand touched Ronan's face.

It was the last thing he knew.

❊❊❊

Emuirdane materialized in the south wing of Draviski castle, in the corridor that led to his wife's bedchambers.

Bloody, frustrated, and in desperate need of release, he stalked down the blood-red carpet, shouting at the first person he spied. "Send the healer to my wife's rooms, and I want her baths readied as well."

He raked the items on a table off to the floor as he passed, ignoring the thousand-year-old Crucian vase as it shattered. "Send three chambermaids and fresh clothing."

The young girl he'd caught in the middle of cleaning draperies huddled into the rich fabric and quaked, her mouth and eyes huge round circles of fear.

"Move you little puss or I'll throw you to my soldiers!"

She cried out and stumbled, fell to her knees.

Emuirdane leaned down and screamed, "Move! Move!" his spittle spraying her face. He grabbed her by the hair and wrenched her to her feet.

She ran, crying, and disappeared around the corner.

Incensed by the ineptitude of all who surrounded him, he continued down the hall, ripping off his ruined coat and flinging it to the floor. He pushed inside Hellana's room, the door bouncing off the wall from the force of his shove.

"Wake up, wife!" Even for her, he could not rein in his temper. Could not summon the endearments he usually tried to lavish upon her. His most beloved.

Still abed—because she was chained there—Hellana jerked to a sitting position. "Emuirdane. What's amiss?"

What she was truly asking was why he had come to disturb her. "I have need of my wife," he told her, removing the black shirt he wore. Another garment ruined by the blade of that Legion warmonger.

His very eyes seemed afire as they combed over her fair beauty. Her ocean-blue hair looked cleaner today. In fact, she looked more kempt than usual.

Yet the abhorrent stench remained. "What is that smell?" Ignoring the odor as it hit his nostrils, he marched to her bed and ripped back her bedcovers. "You look clean enough." Perhaps he didn't need the baths run after all.

He leaned down. Sniffed at her hair. And jerked upright. "Midnight freesia. Your favorite." He narrowed his eyes, scanning her bare arms, her swelling breasts that rose and fell with her panicked breaths. She was freshly groomed.

Suspicion slithered in his mind. He sensed deception. "From

where does the foul odor emanate, my love?" He grabbed a lock of her hair and jerked. "Tell me quick."

She whimpered and tried to pull the blankets back up. "I don't feel well. You know—"

He gripped her chin with his fingers, squeezed until she cried out. "Where?" he demanded, his tone sharp and hard, brooking no more lies.

"It's only my sick bucket under the bed."

He bent to inspect, and instantly clapped a hand over his nose and mouth. Rising again, he crossed the room just as two maids scrambled through the door. "My lord," they said in unison and curtsied.

"Remove the bucket of filth from beneath my wife's bed," he told one. To the other he said, "Clean this blood from my back."

The maid ran to the bathing chamber and returned swiftly with two rags, one wet and soapy, the other dry. As she wiped him down, he slipped from his pants. "All the blood. Make sure you get the inside of my thigh."

As the warm wetness laved his skin, he stared at Hellana. By the time the maid had finished, he was fully erect and near bursting. "Now get out," he told the girl. The other had already gone, taking the putrid-smelling bucket with her.

"And tell the healer I no longer need her." His wound had already knit itself together, barely paining him when he moved.

The door had not even closed behind the maid when he went to the end of the bed and crawled atop the fine periwinkle cover. "My darling," he crooned to Hellana. "How I've missed you."

"Emuirdane, I beg of you. I'm still sick. I can't—"

He put his hand over her mouth, pushed her back into the pillows. "Hush, love. I'll be tender." He considered his foul mood, his raging lust, left unsatisfied for so very long. "Well, as tender as I can manage."

He slipped a hand under her silken gown and squeezed her

breast until she moaned. Pleasure or pain he could not discern. But either aroused him, so it mattered not.

"I can't. No." Hellana continued pleading, even as he gripped the neckline of her gown. She tried to wriggle away until he rent the fabric.

Her hands flew to her stomach then, holding the gown together just below her breasts. "No! Stop this!"

"You are my wife!" He gripped her wrists. "You are my property, bought and paid for with my promise of that damned Ceffyl. All I've endured has been for you." He put his mouth next to her ear and growled, "So you *will* submit."

He sat up, ripped apart her arms, and—went utterly stiff.

Hellana tried again to push him away and said accusingly, "I'm *pregnant.*"

Stunned beyond belief, Emuirdane took in the sight of her rounded belly. He absorbed the impact. "Pregnant?"

Hellana sobbed beneath him and tried to cover herself.

But the foreign mound fascinated him. The markings on her skin. The change in her navel. In one of the rare instances of his long life, Emuirdane was unsure of his own feelings, his own reaction.

How had this never occurred to him? How had he not seen? She was large, surely near the end of her carrying months. But how had she grown so quickly? A mere six weeks ago she was—

Emuirdane arrested his calculations. He'd been so preoccupied with the Ceffyl and the Daughters of Nadia, spent so much time traveling back and forth, that he'd lost track of his own time.

Three months in the mortal world was seven in the Ielonaar realm.

"This is why you've been vomiting?" He studied her blue eyes as they leaked. "*This* is why you've kept me away?"

She bobbed her head and sniffled. "You understand now. We can't have . . . We can't be together in that way." She touched his forearm. "Please, husband. I fear for the babe. Such an act," she swallowed, "especially with your . . . *preferences.* It might cause harm. And also, my body is different, far too sensitive."

Something in her eyes and the way she pleaded twisted inside Emuirdane. Her meekness was so pleasing. Her sweet, beguiling voice, those big blue eyes, wet with tears. They only helped to confirm his decision.

So slowly, he took the tattered edges of her gown in hand.

And slowly, he spread them apart, baring her changed body for his inspection.

"Emuirdane," she pleaded.

With a greedy leer, he slipped a finger inside her mouth. He shifted his body, positioning himself between her legs. "It is my child you carry. A Draviski heir."

Paying no heed to her weeping, he kissed her swollen breast. "I think he can take it."

❈❈❈

One hour later, Hellana lay huddled in her bed. Holding her breath, she listened for the closing of the door to mark her husband's departure. Only after she heard the click of the latch did she gather what was left of her ragged gown and throw it to the floor.

Hot tears of fury and humiliation wet her cheeks as she kicked at the covers and flung pillows across the room.

Everything reeked of Emuirdane. The linens. Her clothing.

Her body.

Fingers spread, she molded her hands over her belly. Naked and exposed, she cried and cried, a seemingly bottomless well of tears. "This is what I deserve. This is what I deserve." She threw back her head, inhaled, and moaned. "But my baby doesn't."

When the door cracked open again, she jumped, a sound of fear bursting from her lips.

But Emuirdane had not returned. It was only Veloria, peeking inside.

Her kind eyes fell upon Hellana, softened with sympathy. She whispered to someone in the hallway before entering the room. "I've sent for the chambermaids. We'll draw you a bath."

Hellana could only nod. Thankfully, her chains allowed her to reach the bathing quarters. If she had to lie all night with Emuirdane's scent choking her . . . reminding her . . .

"I hate him." The words shuddered from her lips, one by one. "I. Hate. Him."

Now her shoulders, arms, and legs began to quiver uncontrollably. But not from fear. Not from sadness.

The pure loathing she felt for her husband seared across her brain like a firestorm, turning her vision and her thoughts a rich and murderous red. "He's a beast. A fiend."

A soft towel draped over her shoulders, and she looked up into Veloria's face. The healer's troubled expression turned Hellana's mind back to her primary concern.

"My babe," she whispered. "What Emuirdane did." She gulped against another bout of weeping as it rose up inside her. Her voice shook. "Will my baby—"

"Shh. Hush now." Veloria soothed Hellana's hair down with loving strokes. "Your bairn is fine."

"How can you be sure?"

"It is my gift to know. My gift to heal." Veloria pursed her lips and adopted a no-nonsense manner. "Do you have pain?"

"No. Not where the baby is." Hellana clenched her eyes shut against the embarrassment, because other parts of her were red and raw, bruising even now.

"Any bleeding?" Veloria asked more softly.

"No."

"Then listen to your healer, for I am old and wise." The older woman teased in an attempt to calm her mistress. "Your bairn is healthy and strong."

Drawing a deep ragged breath, Hellana blew it back out and expelled the bulk of her worry. "Thank you."

Despite her relief, images of what she'd just endured—at her own husband's hands—flashed like sadistic pictures in her head. Then the images changed, and she saw her babe being raised by that monster.

Whether boy or girl, the child would be damaged. They would end up bent and twisted, emotionally deformed by Emuirdane's depravity. They would turn out weak, cowed, and neurotic.

Or, she thought and trembled inside, the child would become the mirror image of its father.

"I can't stay here," she said suddenly.

Veloria sat beside her. She took Hellana's hand. "No. You can't."

Hellana tilted her head in surprise. She'd expected the healer to argue, to try and dissuade her from such dangerous talk. Everyone in the castle answered to Emuirdane.

And no one would go against her husband's orders.

No one other than Veloria.

"You must escape," the healer insisted. "I fear for you and the bairn. After tonight." She shook her head and lowered her voice. "Such rage cannot always be controlled. One day, I'm afraid—"

"He'll go too far." Hellana leaned over, resting on the old woman's shoulder. "I fear that as well."

"Then it is settled." Veloria patted her hand and rose. "I'll put together a plan, but it must be soon." She dropped her gaze to Hellana's stomach. "The end of your term grows near."

"Soon." Both terror and hope lifted inside of Hellana. Escape from Castle Draviski was near impossible.

But Veloria had served Emuirdane's father. She'd grown up here and knew the secrets of the fortress better than anyone.

"When?" Hellana asked, scooting off the bed, unconcerned

when the towel fell and left her standing nude. "When can we go?"

"Soon, my dove. Soon." Veloria winked and notched her head toward the bathing chamber. "But first let's get you cleaned up." The old woman lifted her chin. "Flowered soaps and oils. They will rid you of his scent."

Hellana sighed as hope began to win out over fear. She had at least one person in her corner, one person who truly cared.

And one person was more than she'd had in years.

"A warm bath scented with flowers." She took the healer's soft, wrinkled hand. "Then I can sleep."

"Yes, my dove." Veloria caressed Hellana's cheek. "Then you, and the babe, can sleep in peace."

16

"Fiona! Get away from him!"

Fiona jerked her head up when Sami shouted. She ignored the ire, the revulsion, in her sister's glare and strove for calm. "Help me get him to the car."

"What?" Sami rushed over, leaned down and grabbed Fiona's arm. "What the hell are you doing? Leave him. Let's go."

"No!" Fiona jerked free.

A few steps behind Sami, Tate came to a sudden stop. "Oh, my God. Is that who I think it is?" She looked as perplexed as Sami did angry. "What happened here?"

"Emuirdane," Fiona said. The name was explanation in itself. "Please, there's no time. We have to get him home to Mom. She knows more about spells and potions than any of us and is the only one who might be able to help him."

"Fuck that." Sami crossed her arms, her eyes shooting daggers down at the unconscious Ronan. "Call an ambulance if you want. Let them deal with him."

"You know they can't help him!" Fiona cried. She cradled Ronan's head in her lap—his face white as chalk and breaths far too shallow.

His injury was critical and there was no time for confrontation. So she focused her attention on her sensible sister. "Tate, please. It's complicated, I know, and I swear to tell you everything. But just trust me now. We *have* to save him."

Tate gave the slightest shake of her head, and Fiona knew that she, like Sami, was remembering the last time they'd seen Ronan—the explosions, the deadly fall.

The day he'd tried to murder them.

Before Tate could refuse, Fiona played her trump card. The only card she had. "He can bring us the Ceffyl. We'll never find her without him."

Tate's dark eyes whipped to Fiona's face. "What are you talking about?"

"He can summon the horse. Now, please! He's dying!"

Tate lifted her shoulders as if still struggling to decide.

But then Sami cursed under her breath, shocking Fiona when she kneeled on Ronan's opposite side and hooked her arm under his. "Tate, get his feet," she snapped.

People were beginning to stop and stare, so Sami added loudly for their benefit, "We have to get him to the doctor."

Wracked by gratitude and relief, Fiona sighed and said, "Thank you." Her voice cracked and tears threatened, so she hardened herself, clamping down on the emotions. She couldn't help Ronan if she dissolved into a blubbering mess.

"Wait." She clambered over to pick up his weapon and the pack still lying on the grass. With both his bag and hers slung over one shoulder, she rejoined her sisters. Together, they hefted his dead weight.

"He's heavy," Sami groaned. "All that stupid Legion muscle." She huffed and puffed, as they all did, then muttered, "Magick. Use it."

Of course. Fiona should have thought of that. As one, she and her sisters channeled their ability for telekinesis and Ronan's body lightened significantly. Once they made it to the car, Sami was able to reach out and open the door.

"I'll sit with him," Fiona said and started to climb into the back seat.

"No." Sami's bark froze her in place. "If this asshole wakes up, you aren't going to be the one holding him."

Sami got in and lugged Ronan with her. "Tate, you drive. Fiona, call home and tell them what's happening."

Arguing would only slow them down, so Fiona jumped in the front, pulled her phone from her bag, and hit dial. When her mother answered the call, she sent up a small prayer of thanks. "Mom, we're on our way home. We need your help. We have a man who was struck by Emuirdane's magick."

"Fiona." Tate pursed her lips and sent her a sidelong glance.

"Mom," Fiona gulped and admitted, "it's Ronan. The warrior from Faerie." Her mother fell completely silent, and Fiona readied herself to convince her as she had Tate and Sami.

"Bring him to the side door. To the kitchen." Her mother's tone was steady and practical. "We'll be ready."

Fiona hung up. And now the tears started to push their way through. "It's all my fault. All of it."

Tate sighed heavily but made no comment.

And for once, neither did Sami.

They drove the rest of the way in a thick, tense silence, Fiona glancing back every few seconds to make sure Ronan was still breathing. When they pulled into the drive, her anxiety ratcheted back up.

Brit and Jack stood waiting outside.

"Don't let them hurt him," Fiona whispered to her sisters. "You have to give me a chance to explain."

"Oh, we will." Sami opened the door once Tate skidded to a halt. "I can't *wait* to hear this story."

Fiona was out the door and standing protectively when the men walked over. "Be gentle with him," she commanded.

"Be gent—" Brit began. But then he broke off, stared hard at Fiona, and shared a knowing look with Jack. "Shit," he said. "Why didn't we see this coming?"

Jack heaved a breath and frowned down at Ronan. "Let's just get him taken care of."

Fiona sent her brother-in-law a weak smile. "Thank you."

"That way we can get some answers out of him before kicking his ass back through the portal."

"Okay, okay." Tate waved her hands. "Revenge is going to have to wait." The words had barely left her mouth when their mother leaned out the door and called, "Bring him in."

Everyone fell into action at once, the men taking the bulk of Ronan's weight, with a little magickal help from Sami and Fiona. Tate, meanwhile, ran ahead to talk to their mother.

They entered the side door directly into the kitchen where the long wooden table had been cleared off. Several of the colorful bottles from their mother's collection were lined up, along with various crystals.

Fiona recognized the clear quartz point and amethyst cluster for healing, and a polished obelisk of smoky quartz to help remove negative energy. She appreciated seeing blue banded agate as well, a stone to alleviate pain and calm anxiety.

The last wasn't necessary for physical restoration, but Fiona shouldn't have expected any less from her mother. Innately compassionate and kind to all, she not only intended to heal Ronan's body, but to soothe his injured spirit as well.

Brit and Jack lowered Ronan to the table, and Fiona rushed to her mother's side. "Emuirdane hit him with lightning, green-tinted, full of his magick. Ronan was right on top of him. He took it all in his shoulder and fell. He just fell."

"All right. Settle down." Her mother took Fiona by the shoulders. Briskly, she spoke to Tate and the others. "Remove his clothing so I can have a better look." Releasing Fiona, Nadia bent over her patient and began her assessment.

With capable but tender hands, she lifted Ronan's eyelids, checking his pupils one at a time. Felt his pulse. Monitored his breathing. At last, she nodded to herself as though confirming something.

But when Jack sliced through Ronan's shirt to reveal his chest, Nadia gave a small gasp.

Blackish-green streaks marred Ronan's chest and left arm, as if decay had spread from the wound and was gradually rotting its way through his body.

Fiona bit her bottom lip to keep from crying out, and instantly tasted the copper of blood.

"It's as if he's been poisoned." Nadia clasped her fingers together, her thumbs jittering as her mind worked for an answer. "His heart rate is already too low, so I can't stop the spread by slowing it down further."

She shook her head. "I don't know enough about Emuirdane's magick or how it's attacking the tissues and cells." She studied Ronan's prone form before exhaling and turning to Fiona. "I'm not sure I can help him."

"You have to try."

"I will, but," she took Fiona by both shoulders, "listen to me. I can't promise that anything I do will be enough to save him."

"She said he can summon the Ceffyl," Tate put in. "If that's true—"

"Of course it's true." Fiona snapped at her sister mid-sentence. "But even if it weren't . . ."

She faced her mother again. "Please. Just try."

Nadia put her palm against Ronan's forehead. Her tone was solemn when she said, "I'll do what I can."

Fiona nodded and moved to sit by Ronan, taking his hand in hers. She didn't miss the stunned expressions and mutinous glances, but at the moment, she honestly didn't care.

All she could think of was the pain she'd felt when the cretid had stung her, how the burning agony had seared into her, turning the whole world black.

Now Ronan was the one suffering. Their roles had been reversed, and she was responsible for his wellbeing.

And while her mother might be a talented healer, Fiona had something equally important.

Faith.

Faith in Ronan and their shared destiny. Faith that their mission would not end here. Faith that together, they would bring the Ceffyl back.

Whatever it took, she would return the balance. She would save his life.

Just as he had once saved hers.

Standing straight, she cleared her voice and firmed her resolve. Scanning the implements along the table she asked, "What more can we do? Another crystal? More candles?" She picked up a blue candle with an inscription and noticed the green healing candles had none.

"Now that you've seen him," she said to her mother, "is there anything—"

Nadia took the candle from her, ran a finger over the inscription. "Yes. There just might be." She barked an order to Sami, sending her up to the attic to retrieve another green candle. "And bring my scribing tool," she called after her.

"Jack, stoke the fire, please. Build it up so we can keep him warm." Nadia placed her thumb to her mouth as if in thought. "The poison is the thing. If we can stave it off in any way, prevent sepsis and keep his system from crashing . . ."

She met Fiona's worried stare. "We might have a chance. But a small one," she added quickly when Fiona put a fist to her chest in hope.

"I understand." With the others performing various tasks, Fiona leaned down and spoke softly to Ronan. "I know you can hear me, Ronan. You're too strong and too stubborn to let a little bit of poison slow you down."

She touched his forehead and trembled at the intense heat of his skin. Smoothing back his deep brown hair, she continued to murmur. To soothe and encourage.

Sami returned and gave the requested items to their mother. She, in turn, inscribed Ronan's name into the green wax, along with a symbol Fiona didn't recognize.

At her questioning look, Nadia explained, "It's means antidote. It should help some."

Fiona leaned down to Ronan again. "It's my turn to save you," she whispered, kissing his cheek. "And I don't intend to fail."

Across the room, Brit made a sound of frustration. Fiona threw him a glare and would have replied.

But Ronan groaned and rolled his head to the side.

"Ronan?" Fiona rubbed his fingers in hers, spoke near his face. "Ronan, wake up and talk to me."

His eyelids fluttered and then opened wide. "Fiona. Where—"

"You're safe. I've brought you home." She squeezed his hand. "My mother is taking care of you. We all are," she said, the expression she cast around the room daring anyone to disagree.

Nadia sat on the other side of him. "The blow you took sent poison into your body. "I'm trying what I can to—"

Ronan grabbed her mother's wrist.

Brit, Jack, and Sami all lurched forward.

"In my bag," Ronan said, barely audible. "The dark brown phial. Crystals."

Fiona's mother made a halting motion to the others and lowered her head to hear better.

Ronan gritted his teeth as if in pain. "Place one in the center of the wound. Work outward . . . in a spiral. Counter-clockwise."

"All right." Nadia began to step away, but Ronan held her in his grasp.

"Once they turn black, put the crystals back in the phial. Important . . ." He closed his eyes but continued to speak, straining on each word. "Don't. Throw. Them. Out."

"I'll do as you say," Nadia assured him. "Now rest." She left him and went to Tate who was already combing through Ronan's leather pack.

Granddad chose that moment to walk in, his silver hair in disarray. Evidence he'd just woken from his midday nap. He blinked several times as if trying to clear the strange sight before him. A half-naked man on his kitchen table and a general sense of controlled chaos.

After a pause, he thrust his cane toward Ronan. "Who's this?"

Brit answered, "That would be Ronan." Though he still addressed his father, his eyes settled on Fiona. "The man from Faerie we told you about. Remember? The one who tried to kill us all."

"Well," Granddad pulled back his cane, "what in the bloody hell is he doing here?" He tapped his cane. "And bleeding on my antique table."

"Dad." Nadia carried an oval bottle, the glass a dark brown. "He's not a threat, and before we do anything, anything at all, Fiona has much to share with us." For the first time, a hint of recrimination entered her mother's eyes. "Isn't that right, Fee?"

With a slight nod, Fiona whispered, "Yes."

Granddad continued to grumble, but he made his way across the kitchen to stand beside Brit. Then, as if having second thoughts, he went to the stove and picked up the copper kettle to fill with water. "I'll be needing a cup of tea to get through this."

Still holding Ronan's hand, Fiona watched her mother pour small chunks of pink crystal from the phial Ronan had instructed her to find. She placed one in the center of his black, weeping wound and, despite his grimace, set the others on his tainted flesh.

One by one, she laid the crystals out in the counterclockwise spiral. On his torso, shoulder, and arm, atop the putrid streaks snaking outward like one huge, lethal star.

While Nadia tended to the toxic injury, Ronan angled his face to Fiona.

The smile she would have offered froze on her lips.

"An Iele," he said, the words coated thick with disgust. "You can't give him the Ceffyl, Fiona."

"Just rest," she said, the attempt at comfort lodging in her throat, trapped there by a great mass of shame. She could just imagine what he must think of her now. "You need to heal. We'll talk after. I promise."

"You can't turn the Ceffyl over to him." His amber eyes were as hard and cold as the stone itself. "You *won't* give it to him," he told her in a low, harsh voice, his furious gaze never wavering.

Fiona gulped as remorse twisted its blade.

"Because I won't let you." Though he was weak, Ronan pulled his hand from hers.

And Fiona's heart twinged, as if it had cracked.

Her mother pressed a palm to Ronan's forehead and murmured an incantation.

Then quickly—blessedly—he fell into a deep sleep.

17

"Okay, let's go," Sami demanded.

Fiona hadn't even closed the door to the guest room where Ronan had been moved to recuperate. Though her mother had deemed his condition much improved, Fiona didn't feel right about leaving him alone.

Her family, however, would no longer be put off. Even now Jack and Brit waited for her beside Sami, and all three had her in their crosshairs.

"All right. All right." Fiona kept her voice low and shooed Sami away from the door.

Sami rolled her eyes. "God forbid we disturb the assassin."

"He's not an assassin," Fiona whispered, already marching down the steps with the certain knowledge the others would follow. And they did.

Her family was justified in their anger, but Fiona had reasons for her secrecy. As she walked, she fortified herself, hardening her usually sensitive feelings and rolling back her shoulders. By the time she reached the kitchen, she felt prepared for the interrogation to come.

But when she walked in, she looked at the table where Ronan had lain. And just like that, emotional exhaustion swamped her.

A breath seeped from her lungs, as if she'd been holding it there since she'd first spotted Emuirdane in the park, and every bit of her energy drained, sapping whatever defenses remained. All the twists and turns of the previous week tumbled one upon the other, too much to bear after the day's tragedy.

Standing in the middle of the kitchen, she simply covered her eyes to block it all out.

And she was still there, face buried in her palms, when she felt gentle hands grip her shoulders. "Come. Sit down." Her mother's voice, soft with concern.

Fiona nodded and dropped her arms. Her mother and Tate had obviously been busy, clearing the table and setting the kitchen to rights. And instead of launching his inquiry, Brit moved to the counter for coffee, while Sami searched the pantry for snacks.

Despite all Fiona had done, her family was still looking out for her. Taking care when she could not.

"You should all be furious with me," she said meekly.

Granddad came over and patted her cheek. "Oh, we are. Don't you worry." He winked. "But we've got eyes in our heads, don't we? We can see whatever's gone on has taken its toll."

"We can be upset you with, Fee," Brit said, pausing halfway to the filter with a scoop of grounds. "But that doesn't mean we stop loving you."

"And loving you," Sami slapped a box of ginger thins on the table, "means you're not getting out of this kitchen. Not until you spill your guts."

Fiona sent her sister a weak smile. "I know." Then, too tired to continue standing, she ambled over to sit near the fire. A chill had crept into her bones, and she just couldn't get warm.

When the kettle screeched atop the stove, she startled and put her fingers to her temples. "Ronan must be so disappointed in me."

Though she'd spoken low and under her breath, Sami, of course, heard every word. "Uh . . . what?" Her sister made a sound in her throat. "You're worried about *him* being disappointed?" She dropped into a chair and dragged the box of ginger cookies over to her. "I think I'll take these back."

A cup of hot tea appeared before Fiona, and she could tell by the scent her mother had prepared her favorite. Raspberry Earl. "Why don't we all just listen? Quietly," Nadia added, casting a sharp eye toward Sami, "and let Fiona start from the beginning."

With coffee brewing and flames snapping in the hearth, some of the tension left Fiona's body. Surrounded by her family, shielded by their presence, she sent her mind back to that first day and the phone call that had started it all.

By the time she'd downed her cup of tea and devoured six ginger thins, they'd heard all about Mr. Walsh and how he'd found the Ceffyl, stabling and caring for the horse over the winter months.

She'd told them how Ronan had barged into the stables, and of those first days of animosity when he'd forced her to keep his presence a secret. Then she'd shocked them with details of Aurellia, and how a meeting with a goddess had changed her views.

"I know exactly what you're all feeling, because I didn't trust Ronan either. To be totally honest," Fiona gave a little shrug, "I was scared of him."

Sitting beside her, Nadia leaned in and wrapped her in a hug. "Yet you went with him to another world and stood before a goddess you feared might punish you." She squeezed Fiona as if she'd never let go. "Oh, my sweet, brave girl."

Now Fiona focused on Sami and Brit, as they seemed to be the holdouts, the only two still watching her through narrowed eyes. "Ronan being here, the Dea Matrona's involvement, our working together. It's all sudden for you, and I get that."

Fiona exhaled with a touch of laughter. "Believe me, I do. But once Ronan and I learned we were meant to work together, I could see he was relieved. He never wanted to hurt me."

She glanced around at Brit, Jack, and her sisters. "He never wanted to hurt *any* of us."

Brit scoffed and furrowed his brow. "You could have fooled me. Because he sure seemed to be doing his damnedest on that bridge."

"Oh, but that was just him doing his *duty*." Sami made air quotes when she said the last.

Fiona's tone grew defensive. "Yes. He was doing his duty. He was defending Jewel, an innocent creature that he believed would be ill-used by any who possessed her."

"Jewel?" Tate asked, her brows lifting to her hairline. "You named the horse?"

Ignoring the question, Fiona asked instead, "Wouldn't we all do the same? Wouldn't we want to protect the Ceffyl as well? I think so. I think we would fight to keep it out of Emuirdane's hands, but we can't while he's got a knife to our throat."

"So what are you saying?" Sami stood and crossed to refill her coffee cup. "That giving the Ceffyl to Emuirdane is the wrong thing to do?"

Fiona's spine went rigid. "Maybe that's exactly what I mean. The more he threatens, the less I want to hand over that much power."

"The less you want to hand over Jewel." Tate had latched on to one very telling point. Fiona had not only given the horse a name, but she also continued to use it.

"She's a living being who's been swept up into human and Fae controversy for far too long. A fact that even the Dea Matrona regrets."

When Tate opened her mouth to reply, Fiona rushed on. "Knowing that, Emuirdane is the last being who should control the Ceffyl. Plus, with the way he holds the contract over our heads, there's no guarantee he will leave us alone once we give him the Ceffyl."

Fiona was on a roll now, so she turned to her mother. "We all know how evil he is. How . . . *greedy*. We have rare powers, strong enough that we survived the trials of Mount Aeylwon when none had before. Human or Fae. So who's to say Emuirdane won't decide to call on us again? Force us into doing his dirty work whenever he pleases?"

"And we still won't be able to fight his magick," Sami said heatedly. "He's stronger than us, and if we don't give him the horse, he will be royally pissed off. We don't know what he'd do then, but that's a chance I don't want to take."

At Sami's words, Fiona flashed back to that day on the road. When Emuirdane had glamoured her, made her experience a crash, pain. And paralysis.

"There's just no good answer, is there? Every choice leads to disaster." And the reality of that, the unfairness of it all, flooded her system with rage.

"Look," Fiona said, "I'm not excusing my actions. I'm just trying to explain Ronan's perspective. He had a terrible decision to make on that bridge, but ultimately, he honored the oath he'd taken."

Now it was Fiona's turn to rise from the table. "A *sacred* oath." As she filled her cup with fresh hot water, a revelation hit. She was repeating the same logic Ronan had used. Almost verbatim.

Because at some point in their time together, she'd come to understand his side of things. She'd come to respect him, to admire him. And possibly more.

She remembered the brief but thrilling kiss in the library, the way his strong arms had enfolded her. How they'd made her feel secure. She floated in the memory, lost in its sweetness.

And then her grandfather's voice broke through the reverie. "So because of your involvement with the man, Emuirdane tried to kill him today."

Fiona spun around, her expression turning grim. "Yes. He would have ended Ronan. If I hadn't stepped in."

"You risked your life for the warrior," Jack said, running a hand through his dark blonde hair.

"No. Not really." Fiona dunked a new teabag in her cup as she returned to sit. "We all know Emuirdane won't kill us. He can threaten all he wants, but he has to keep us dangling by that same string. He can't transform the horse, so he needs us to do it for him."

She sipped her tea, musing silently for a moment. "I didn't risk my life today." She brought her gaze up to meet those of her family. "But Ronan risked his. Without a second thought, he put himself between Emuirdane and me. He protected me."

Her hand shook so she gripped her cup, let the warmth settle in. "And now he knows I've been deceiving him too."

She let the impact of her statement sink in before steering the topic back to herself. Back to her own behavior. "I'm sorry I lied to all of you." Setting aside her tea, she curled her fingers into fists atop the wood. "Deceiving the people I cherish most has been one of the hardest things I've ever done. I know I worried you, and I hate that. But if I had to do it all again . . . I would."

Sami expelled a breath and stared down into her lap.

"And wouldn't you, Sami?" Fiona asked. "Brit? Wouldn't any one of you have done the same if it meant keeping the family safe? Every time the guilt came close to doing me in, I reminded myself what was at stake. If Ronan had taken the Ceffyl . . ."

"Emuirdane would have taken his revenge," Granddad said, his eyes filled with empathy. "He would have hurt or killed one of us."

He gripped the handle of his cane. "I have a bit of experience with the guilt you're speaking of, as I'm the one who made the deal with Emuirdane." His eyes took on a faraway look.

"Dad," Nadia began, then stopped when he held up a finger.

"Not to worry. I'm not back to blaming myself." Granddad gave his full attention to Fiona. "I just know how it feels to have one choice look as bad as the other, if only in hindsight."

He got up from the table and took a few steps toward the door before pivoting back. "None of us asked to have our lives tangled up with gods and faeries, but this is where we are now. Fiona did what she felt best, and she did it to safeguard the rest of us. I have my reservations about the man upstairs."

He looked upward, as if he could see Ronan through the floors above his head. Then he let his blue gaze move from person to person. "But if the goddess has given her blessing, who am I—who are any of us—to tell her nay?" He tilted his head to one side and shrugged. "I don't mind knowing she's still on our side, for that means we are still on the side of righteousness."

He waggled his cane at them. "And now I'm off for a short evening nap. The day's events have drained me dry."

Fiona and the others watched him go, and for a moment after his departure the only sound heard was the hiss and crackle of flames in the hearth.

Finally, Brit spoke. "I just need a little more time to wrap my head around it, but Dad's got a point. If the Dea Matrona says Fiona and Ronan were destined to meet, in whatever manner, then I have to consider the bigger picture."

Sami still looked disgruntled, but at least she was listening, cheek resting in her palm as she faced her uncle.

"The only question," Brit continued, "is what will happen if you succeed in returning the horse to its inanimate form. Is Ronan still determined to take the Ceffyl back to Faerie?" He looked around the table. "Because we will have Emuirdane to contend with. He may have let Ronan live, but he still expects us to hold up our end of the bargain."

Fiona could give him no satisfactory answer, so she only nodded.

"I think we can put off that problem, at least for today," Nadia told her brother. "Once Ronan is healed, we can worry about what comes next."

Brit cocked his head, started to speak, and then seemed to change his mind. He rose and took his dirty mug to the dishwasher. He returned but didn't sit, standing next to Fiona. "I've rescheduled a meeting at the bank, and I don't want to make them wait any later than they have." He cracked a grin for Fiona. "I'm to sign the papers for the Morrison Building. I assume you still want to be my tenant?"

A shard of Fiona's anxiety shattered and fell away. "Do you still want me?"

He chucked her chin. "Of course I do." His countenance turned serious. "But promise me you'll watch yourself around the warrior. Until we know what he intends—"

"I will," Fiona said quickly. "I'll be careful. I promise," she added when he only continued to stare down at her.

At last, his features relaxed. "He's not the only one who feels protective, you know. So give us a little leeway."

Fiona stood and hugged her uncle. "I know. And I'm sorry I lied to you the other morning."

"And every other day," Sami pointed out. She seemed to be taking the betrayal harder than anyone else, so Fiona pulled away from Brit and faced her sisters.

She had a feeling the discussion wasn't over.

Brit tossed up a hand in farewell and exited out the side door. With the other men gone, Tate gave Jack a small nudge with her elbow.

"Huh?" he asked with a baffled expression for his wife.

Tate inclined her head to indicate the door.

"Oh. Right." Jack jumped up. "Time to go." He ruffled Fiona's hair as he passed and made a hasty exodus right behind Brit.

"We need to know something," Tate said, getting straight to the point. She drew a breath, glanced at Sami and Nadia, and asked, "Are your feelings for Ronan going to be a problem?"

Fiona didn't bother to deny the truth of her sister's words, nor did she evade the question. Because she just couldn't lie anymore. Not to them, to Ronan. Or to herself.

"No," she said plainly, grasping the back of the chair. "There are greater powers at work in all of this, and I'm coming to accept that. I trust all of you, and I always will." She paused, hoping her next statement wouldn't hurt them. "But I have to start relying on myself, on my own judgment."

"Looks like you've been doing that already," Sami said. "And that's not a criticism," she added when Fiona frowned. "In fact, I can see the changes in you. I'm not happy you kept us in the dark, especially when you left to go to a farworld."

Sami let that hang in the air a moment. Then she said, "But I have to admit, you seem more . . ."

"Confident," Tate said with a little smile. "And I think it suits you."

Mystified by the compliments instead of the condemnation she'd expected, Fiona quirked a brow and said only, "Uh . . . thanks."

Fiona's mother reached out and took Fiona's fingers in her own. "Why don't you go up and lie down for a while? I can tell you're tired."

Fiona let her shoulders sag. "I really am. I haven't been sleeping very well."

"Then go get some rest. We'll wake you for dinner."

"Yeah, go to sleep," Sami said, but her tone was playful. "Give us time to talk about you behind your back."

Well beyond tired and deep into the land of almost-comatose, Fiona stifled the yawn that suddenly rose up. "Okay. I think I will." Sami had been teasing, but Fiona knew as soon as she walked up the stairs, her sisters and mother would indeed be discussing her.

Her, Ronan, the Ceffyl, the goddess, and of course, Emuirdane. The litany of all the parties involved only served to hammer at the headache Fiona was already fighting, so she took her mother's advice and went upstairs.

But she didn't go to her own room. She slipped inside Ronan's instead.

Color had returned to his cheeks, and his respirations were even and full. He seemed to be resting comfortably enough, though he looked out of place beneath the white quilt with its dainty yellow flowers.

The crystals he'd instructed her mother to use had worked

better than she'd expected. The dark streaks had dissipated, and his wound had shrunk right before their eyes.

But Fiona wouldn't stop worrying until he woke up and . . . and what? Told her how much he despised her? Severed their partnership? Left her to summon the Ceffyl on his own?

No. He wouldn't do those things, because above all else, Ronan was honorable. And he would stay with Fiona until their destinies were fulfilled. Even if he hated her, he would remain.

And so would she.

A chair sat in the corner, so she dragged it over to the head of the bed. A lamp burned low on the table, so she turned it off. The sun was near setting, so the room went dark.

For the longest time, Fiona sat there, listening to Ronan's breathing, touching his arm, and giving thanks that he'd survived.

When her lids began to droop, she leaned over to rest her head on his good shoulder.

And for the first time in weeks, fell straight to sleep.

18

Ronan woke to a light pat on his cheek. Still groggy, he blinked to clear the fog from his mind as well as his eyes. When his vision crystallized, he found a black-haired woman smiling at him and holding up a steaming spoon.

He vaguely recalled having broths and soups slipped into his mouth, over how many hours he could not say. But when the woman said, "You're awake," her familiar voice brought it all rushing back.

"You're Fiona's mother," he said, his unused vocal chords sounding raspy and dry.

"Call me Nadia," she said, offering the spoon. "My special beef stew."

The raised blinds in the windows revealed a land darkening as it fell to dusk, and Ronan rubbed his forehead where a dull ache throbbed. He must have been asleep for hours.

He pushed up to a sitting position and put a hand to the bandage on his shoulder. Feeling no pain, he peeled back the white gauze. A pink mass of scar tissue was all that remained. "How did I heal so fast?"

Brows beetled in confusion, he looked to Nadia. "How long have I been here?"

She put the uneaten spoonful back in the red bowl she held. "Three days."

Ronan jerked his head, and immediately regretted the action

when a starburst ignited behind his eyes. "Three days?"

"Yes."

"Where is Fiona?" he asked.

"Oh, she's been here. For the first two days I had to push her out, or she'd never have gotten any sleep and food for herself." She offered him the bowl. "You look better and more alert. I suspected you were coming around this morning when you sat up and drank an entire glass of orange juice." She laughed. "Then promptly dropped back to the pillow again."

"I think I remember that. My apologies if I've been a difficult patient." And he was about to sound even more difficult, if not downright rude, but he had to know. "So *where* is Fiona?"

The last thing he remembered was staring into the green of her eyes as pain engulfed one side of his body. He'd told her he would stop her. But from doing what? Some parts were still cloaked in a haze.

As the gaps filled in, he recalled how angry he'd been. He'd told Fiona he wouldn't let her give the Ceffyl to . . . "The Iele."

He almost leapt from the bed when the image of the dark Fae came crashing in, but movement made him acutely aware of his state of undress. He lifted the sheet and discovered he wore the fitted boxers he'd come to prefer while in this world.

But nothing else.

"Fiona's fine," Nadia said. "And no, she is not with Emuirdane. However . . ."

Ronan's skin prickled. "What? However what?"

"Hmm." She studied him with eyes almost as deep in color as her hair. "Eat some stew, and I'll tell you why I came. Why I woke you. But," she patted his elbow, "you can relax. She's in no immediate danger."

Ronan knew the look of a mother who would not be dissuaded from administering care, so he scooped large bites into his mouth and downed the glass of water held out.

But before he could ask, yet again, about Fiona, Nadia sat back in the chair and said, "Tate and Sami tell me that you and Fiona have a connection. That the very moment your eyes met, something passed between you."

Caught off guard, he waited several beats before answering. But yes, what she said was correct, and something had passed between them.

Like a silent thunderclap.

But Ronan didn't give voice to the memory, only one slow nod of affirmation.

With a chuckle, Fiona's mother folded her hands in her lap. "Well, this is like pulling teeth. So I'm going to ask you flat out." She stared hard at Ronan. "Do you care for her? Not as the woman the goddess has partnered you with, but as—"

"Yes," Ronan said suddenly, willing to tell her what she wanted, what she apparently needed to hear, so he could find out why she'd come. If he'd been resting and healing for three days straight, then whatever she'd woken him for had to be important.

And it had to do with Fiona.

"Good. I can see you're telling the truth. But I needed to hear it for myself before I sent you out after her."

"Out after her?" Ronan made a false start again and almost threw the covers back. But he caught himself just in time. Healer or not, this was Fiona's *mother*.

And he refused to prance around in front of her in nothing but his skivvies.

"There's a full moon tonight." Nadia gazed out the window and the fallen darkness beyond. "Strong energy for charging spells." Her eyes slammed into Ronan again. "She was able to collect the blood of Rhydderch's line while you were recovering. And she's gone now for the graveyard dirt."

"If she's not in danger, why are you waking me? Why are you telling me this?"

Nadia gave him a knowing smile. "I think it's only fair that you take part in fulfilling your destiny. That, and," she stood and edged toward the door, "I don't want her out there alone in the dark."

"You could have sent her sisters."

"I could have," Nadia agreed. And didn't elaborate.

"Wait," Ronan said when she opened the door. "I need to know. Does your family serve the Iele?"

She took her time before replying, as if deciding how much to tell him. "You and Fiona should talk, but the short answer is no. We are indebted to the Fae, a contract our family has been burdened with since I was an infant."

"So you don't conspire with Emuirdane?"

Her laugh was scornful. "Hardly."

"Then will you ..." Ronan was taking a leap here, but his instincts told him he could trust Nadia Whiteburn. And he needed to go after Fiona. "Will you help me with something?"

Curiosity bloomed in her eyes, and she stepped closer. "That depends."

"When I was hurt, you were there, and I remember you saying you didn't understand his magick. The Iele's." Ronan held the sheet against his waist. "But if you did, would you know better how to combat it?"

"Possibly. But what do you suggest?"

Ronan gestured to his brown phial, sitting atop a bureau. "You kept the crystals?"

"Just as you asked."

"The material absorbs magick, holds it in a kind of stasis." He could tell by the turn of Nadia's head that she was intrigued. "We use them in Faerie," he explained, "to capture and study the lethal powers of the Fae."

"So you're saying we have a sample of Emuirdane's magick?" Now Nadia's smile was full of triumph.

Ronan nodded. "Fiona told me that you were the authority on

spells and charms. That you could be rather . . . creative."

"That I can." Her dark eyes gleamed, and in that instant, Ronan knew he'd found an ally.

Fiona's mother spoke in a conspiratorial whisper. "The next time Emuirdane shows his face—"

Ronan finished her thought. "We'll be ready."

❈❈❈

Moonlight sliced through the winter-bare trees, painting headstones and grass a pale, pale blue. The wind carried an extra chill in the absence of the sun, its whisper the only sound.

Until a bird screeched from a branch high above, startling Fiona as it launched into the air. She followed the path of the dark silhouette as it arced into the sky toward the huge white orb.

The moon's lunar beauty shone bright tonight, casting her power to the land below, making it the perfect time to work the spell. To prepare the gemstones for the Ceffyl's transformation.

Cold slithered through Fiona now, but the arctic ripple had nothing to do with wind or weather. Frozen blocks seemed lodged in her chest, twin bergs of doubt and uncertainty. They'd grown larger over the last few days as she'd questioned her own intentions, and wrestled with her morals.

Should she give the Ceffyl to Emuirdane? Or should she step back and let Ronan's will prevail? If he took the statuette back to Mount Aeylwon, at least the horse would be safe again.

And Ronan would return to his duty, to his life in Faerie. A world away from her.

Another twinge of fear cracked through the ice.

But then she chastised herself for such trivial concerns, especially in the face of much bigger problems.

There was no questioning the scroll from the goddess or the potion's instructions. She just wished the directions had gone a bit farther, far enough to take the decision from her hands.

But wasn't that the whole point? The Ceffyl's fate was bound to hers and Ronan's, and only their choices could bring it to completion. Strength. Intuition. Heart. That's what the Dea Matrona had said.

But even those three things were left open to interpretation.

"Just get this done," Fiona told herself, trudging through the overgrown weeds in search of a grave. The ancient markers were timeworn and ruined, but that's why she'd chosen this place. She couldn't bring herself to dig near more recent burials.

Finally she halted, deciding one spot was as good as another. She pulled a small spade and glass jar from her satchel, then fell to one knee to gather the dirt.

"What do you think you're doing?"

The low, growling voice came from behind her. She froze as she was, kneeling with the tip of her spade planted in the ground.

"Fiona," he said, the snap of fury in his voice.

She whipped around and looked up. "Ronan?" What was he doing here?

More relieved than she had any right to be, she stood to meet him. Recalling his condition, she gestured to his shoulder. "You should be in bed."

"And miss out on all the fun?" He clenched his jaw. "Or should I say, what's left of it? Since you took it upon yourself to complete our tasks. To fulfill the duty assigned to us *both*."

So he knew she'd gone to collect the blood they needed for the potion. "You were injured. You needed to heal." Her logic seemed to bounce off of his rigid exterior, so she tried a different tack. "How did you find me?"

"Your mother."

"My mother?"

"She let me borrow her car. Even put the address in the GPS."

Fiona angled her head, pressed her lips together. "Uh . . . When did you two become such good friends?"

"About thirty minutes ago." Ronan stepped forward. "But that's not the issue. After what happened in the park with that . . . *Iele*," he said the word with distaste, "you would still venture out here?" He waved a hand to indicate the desolate graveyard. "In the dark? By yourself?"

"So wait." Fiona let the spade dangle from her fingers. "You're worried about me? That's why you're angry?"

"I should be angry about a great many things." His eyes were still as fierce as the last time they'd spoken. But they were no longer cold. "Yet what drove me from the sick bed and into the night was the idea of you putting yourself at risk."

His hand came up, cupped her face. "Damn me, yes. I'm angry because you made me worry. Because I care about you, Fiona. More than I should." He dropped his forehead to hers in a gesture she found endearing. "I have a mission from the goddess, and that should be first in my mind."

He heaved out a breath and retreated several feet. "Instead, you are." He whirled on her, accusation stamped in his features. "I can't tell right from wrong anymore. I find myself second-guessing what should be a foregone conclusion."

Fiona threw the spade down. "Do you think this is easy for me? That I know the answer? All I can do is follow the directions from that cryptex and hope I somehow figure out how to please the goddess, save my family, and come out of this with my conscience intact."

She walked to him and put her hand on his arm, their gazes clashing in the pale moonlight. "So, yes. I went without you to get the blood from Rhydderch's descendant. The man I found wanted nothing to do with me," she scoffed, "or my story. It probably sounded like lunacy to him. Jeweled horses granting wishes. Gods, witches, and evil faeries."

The wrinkle between Ronan's brows eased away. "How did you

convince him?"

"I didn't. His father was there and heard all I said. He knew the story of the Jeweled Ceffyl, a family tale he'd heard since childhood." Fiona recalled the man's words and shivered. "That poor horse," she whispered, feeling the guilt all over again.

"What?" Ronan asked.

"The elder Rhydderch was a little old man who took a razor and willingly spilled his blood. He said he'd gladly give in his ancestor's name, and to 'free that poor horse.' He believes Jewel is trapped in an unnatural existence."

Ronan didn't speak. He only stood there, the wind ruffling his dark hair, and kept his thoughts to himself. If he had a reaction to the old man's opinion, he didn't share it with her.

At length, he put his hand over Fiona's. "Your mother mentioned something about a contract with the Iele."

"Yes. Emuirdane cured my mother from an illness when she was a baby. Only afterwards did he tell my grandfather how the debt was to be paid."

"He tricked him," Ronan said.

Fiona nodded.

"I heard you talk to Emuirdane in the park, after I'd been hit. You told him you needed me to find the Ceffyl."

"I was afraid he would kill you."

Ronan put a finger to her lips. "I know that now, but at the time I thought you'd conspired with him."

"With Emuirdane?" She snarled. "Never. He is evil beyond imagination."

"I've spent many years among the Fae, and even they fear the Iele. So I *can* imagine." Slipping his arms around her, Ronan pulled her to his chest in one fluid motion. "That's why it ripped me inside when I believed you served him. I couldn't align that in my head. How cruel his kind are."

He stroked her cheek. "And how good I know you to be."

His touch was so delicate, Fiona sucked in a breath, leaned into the caress.

"You've been by my bedside, caring for me these last few days. I remember your scent." His voice turned husky. "Like spring wildflowers."

Ronan dipped down, brushed his lips over hers.

The soft, sweet kiss took Fiona's breath.

Then his mouth crushed down on hers, hard and hot, his tongue doing wicked things. He moaned into her, and Fiona went limp, grabbing onto his shoulders so she wouldn't fall.

The heat in her belly swirled deliciously, and she found herself pressing closer, wanting more. He smelled of the rain, a clean, earthy scent, sending need pounding through her as he deepened the kiss.

When he palmed her breast, she gave herself over. More than lust stirred within her, and the knowledge of that truth whispered from her lips. "Ronan," she said, a prayer and a plea.

And when he lowered her down, she knew that truth was love.

❄❄❄

Fiona felt like fire in his arms, like the white flames she so easily conjured. Beautiful, enchanting—and scorching to the touch.

When her head fell to the side, he couldn't help himself. He traced the graceful curve of her neck with his mouth, and drew a sound of pleasure from her pretty pink lips. When her emerald eyes sparkled up at him, he took those lips again, but this time the joining was gentle and slow.

His heart swelled with foreign emotions, and he drew back to whisper, "I need you, Fiona. You can't know how much."

They stared at each other—for the space of a heartbeat—then Ronan reined himself in and recalled where they were. "But no matter how strong that need, I will not take you on the ground."

Her eyes went blank as he rolled to the side. Then he took her hand and helped her up. "Not you, sweet Fiona." Gently, he curled his fingers under her chin, and lifting her face for a final kiss.

"Why is it you always seem to kiss me out of the blue and then stop just as quickly?" Eyes dreamy as she studied him, she released a long sigh.

"A library chair. A graveyard." Ronan feathered his fingers through her silky black hair. "Perhaps I should do better picking the time and place."

She bit her lip. "Then we'll really be in trouble."

A howl cut through the night and the flirtatious light winked out of her eyes. "Bloodhounds." Jerking around, she scanned the dark woods surrounding the cemetery.

"What's a bloodhound?" Ronan asked, on alert simply because she was.

A female voice carried from somewhere beyond the tree line. "Copper! Stop that racket and come inside."

Fiona wilted and seemed instantly abashed. "Or maybe just a hound dog?"

The brief flicker of alarm was enough to spur Ronan into action. "Let's gather the dirt and be on our way. We still have to create the potion."

"You're right. We should get to work." Fiona eyed the moon and nodded. "While she's still shining bright."

19

Ronan stepped into the attic that spanned the length of the Victorian home. Wood shone, brass gleamed, and the scent of lemon filled the air, and as he took in the décor and aura of the room, two things became clear. The inhabitants of the space were most often female.

And those females had worked some very potent magick.

At the opposite end, a round window framed the rising moon and was situated above an antique desk. Tall shelves flanked the desk, holding books, crystals, and a collection of oddities.

The intrigue of an old brass sextant pulled at Ronan, but when Fiona made her way in the opposite direction, he banished curiosity for the task to be performed.

Pausing midway, she clicked on a lamp, illuminating the glass shade and a dance of purple dragonflies. She continued to a tall green hutch, where she stopped and motioned for Ronan to join her.

When he drew close, she ran a loving hand over the smooth, worn wood. "This is my mother's workspace. She's quite accomplished at deciding which herbs, oils, and other ingredients combine to produce the most powerful spells. As if she reads the essence of each, just as you and I would a book."

Fiona shrugged. "I can only interpret her gift as being similar to how I bake. I have my own recipes, created mostly on instinct."

Ronan was well aware of her mother's ability but would save

that conversation until later, after they'd prepared the jewels. Instead, he stayed on topic. "I hope you'll bake for me sometime."

He touched her arm, drew her eyes to his. "While I'm here."

At the mention of his leaving, her expression clouded over. "Before you go back to Faerie." Gaze averted, she perused the items displayed on the hutch. Colorful bottles, dried herbs, a mortar and pestle—the basic requirements for any witch's pantry.

Other implements stocked the shelves, but Ronan focused on the large swatch of corduroy, a yellow bottle of Abramelin oil, and a vial of crimson liquid that was surely blood.

Now that they had the graveyard dirt, they were ready to begin.

Fiona rubbed her hands together and exhaled. "I'll start." She avoided further mention of Ronan's plans or the looming conflict they would soon have to face. She was fully aware of his intentions. She knew his mission remained the same.

Without further direction from the goddess, his oath remained intact. He'd sworn to always defend the Ceffyl, from any and all threats, human or Fae.

And as far as he could tell, Fiona had not changed her mind. She still planned to appease Emuirdane, relinquishing the Ceffyl for the sake of her family.

He didn't want to believe she would truly go through with it, that she'd give the Ceffyl to such a beast.

But at the moment, nothing mattered other than the potion. The horse couldn't pass between worlds in its current form, leaving them no choice but to continue on.

So for now, he pushed aside his worries and watched Fiona as she selected the jar of dirt.

Unscrewing the lid, she scooped out two spoons of soil and transferred them to a deep glass bowl. She sent a quick glance to Ronan—never meeting his eyes—and nodded to the blood. "I think we should both have a hand in this."

Without reply, Ronan picked up the vial, removed the cork, and added the blood from the line of Rhydderch.

Taking the next step, Fiona measured a similar amount of the Abremalin oil. Once she'd finished pouring, she turned to him with a somber face. "Only one more thing."

"The blood of a Legion warrior." Ronan reached for the sharp blade lying on the hutch and, without hesitation, pulled the knife across his palm. He then dripped a fair amount of his own life force into the concoction.

Fiona handed him a bandage before opening a side cabinet. As Ronan wrapped his wound, she retrieved a black velvet bag and loosened its ties.

"This is it." She held her breath, exhaled on a sigh, and emptied the Ceffyl's jewels into the mixture. Having fallen from the statue as it changed to a living horse, the gems were the key component for reverse transformation.

Ronan inclined his head to the bowl. "The scroll instructed to blend the gemstones until well-coated."

Fiona lifted a spatula. "This is made of ash wood, a substance that is aligned with the earth and embodies both male and female energies."

"Appropriate," he said, putting his fingers over hers where they gripped the handle. Half of him expected her to shun his touch.

But she kept her focus on the potion, her small hand still captured by his. Together they turned over the mixture, blending dirt, blood, and oil to cover the jewels.

"Our energies should be as one, to strengthen the magick." Fiona spoke in earnest, and now she did meet his eyes. "And unify our intent."

Ronan held her gaze, felt the tingling flow of power as it swarmed around them. "What is your intent, Fiona? Tell me."

Her lashes fluttered and her bottom lip trembled. "I want to honor the Dea Matrona and the task she has given us. Strength. Intuition. Heart. She said we would need all of these, and that if in doubt, we should turn to each other."

She kept her hand in his and released the spatula. Yet the utensil continued to stir. "I'm turning to you now, Ronan. I'm telling you I want to do what's right." She bit down on the lip that still quivered. "I'm just not sure what that is."

"I'm sure." He lifted her chin, forcing her to look at him. "My entire life has been about protecting the Ceffyl. Keeping her from those who would use her to fulfill their desires, their avarice or thirst for power. And I can tell you without any doubt, she must *not* go to Emuirdane."

The magick they'd created spun around them, whirling in a shimmer of gold, silver, and all the colors of the jewels. With her arms encircling his waist, Fiona closed her eyes, let her head fall back, as the brilliant lights rose up, up—before flowing back down to curl around them like a ribbon.

Bound together that way, he felt her shiver, and drew a ragged breath in response. Then the colors dissolved.

And the connection was gone.

Still in his embrace, Fiona opened her eyes just as the stirring came to a halt.

She gazed up at him a moment longer, started to speak, but then turned away to remove the spatula. "The gems are ready."

Her voice sounded tremulous, as if she'd been affected too. "Now for the wrapping." She picked up the bowl and waited for Ronan to open the corduroy fastened into a sack. Carefully, she poured in the jewels, then he rolled the fabric into a bundle.

"Outside?" he asked, though he knew the answer.

The final step called for moonlight.

Wordlessly, Fiona left him to walk through the attic and down the stairs, all the way to the bottom floor. Once there, they followed the hallway to the back door and exited to the yard.

Grass stretched out to a line of trees, pines and firs still standing green among the leafless hardwoods. The forest created a barrier between the Whiteburn home and the seaside cliffs, the entire area washed white in moonlight.

"There," Fiona said, pointing to a circle of pavers that would be surrounded by blooms in another few weeks. Two benches sat opposite each other, a small white altar situated dead center.

Ronan moved to the altar and set down the roll of corduroy. Glancing upward, he scanned the sky. "Looks clear. Plenty of light."

Fiona only nodded, staring down at the bundle.

Movement at the base of the trees caught both of their attention. "What are they up to?" Fiona asked, taking several steps in the direction of her mother and sisters who'd just exited the forest.

The trio of women glided over the ground, thin mists parting at their feet. Nadia walked ahead of Tate and Sami, holding a flask. Ronan spied the glittering black haze inside the glass, and a shiver of recognition slithered down his neck.

Well aware magick had been done—and that she'd been left out—Fiona put her hands on her hips. "What have you three been doing?" She flung a hand at the flask. "What is that?"

Nadia smiled at Fiona in her eloquent way. "We've been raising sea mists."

Sami put it more plainly. "We needed the salt."

"For what? You're working a spell?" Fiona rattled off questions. "Does this have something to do with the Ceffyl?"

"Yes," Tate said, "and if you'll take a breath, we'll explain." Her eyes flitted to Ronan and back to her sister. "We've been working with Emuirdane's magick."

"Ronan gave us a few tips on Legion chemistry." Sami pointed a finger at him. "Worked like gangbusters, by the way."

"Wait. Wait. Wait." Fiona cocked her head. "When did all this happen?"

"While you were out graveyard shopping," Sami said.

Nadia stepped forward. "We would have involved you, Fiona,

but time was of the essence, and you and Ronan were already busy."

Fiona processed the explanation and nodded. "Yeah. Okay. I understand." She rubbed her temples. "This is just unexpected. The last time you were all together, Ronan was still considered a danger. Sami you didn't even want him in the house. I just never thought . . ."

She trailed off and dropped her hands. "Okay. It's all fine. I'm just glad there was no bloodshed."

"None at all," Nadia replied, holding out the container for her daughter's inspection.

Leaning closer, Fiona exhaled and studied the glistening haze. "So what exactly have you made?"

"A weapon," Ronan said, meeting Nadia's stare. A moment of accord passed between them. "The crystals I asked your mother to use on my injury were created to absorb magick. In this case, Emuirdane's poison."

"With a benign sample, we were able to examine and alter its components." Tate's smile was infectious. "So we can use it against him."

Fiona gaped at them. "You're saying we have a weapon we can use on Emuirdane?"

"Or to protect us from his power," Ronan clarified. "At the very least."

Putting a hand to her chest, Fiona seemed to be at a loss for words. At length, she reached for the flask. "So while I was gone, you all decided to fight Emuirdane?"

Then her green eyes flashed accusation at Ronan. "And to send the Ceffyl back to Faerie?"

"No, sweetheart. We haven't decided anything." Nadia spoke in a tone meant to assuage. "The task handed down by the Dea Matrona is for you and Ronan. We just wanted to give you more options."

"Options is one way to put it." As she clutched the glass

container to her chest, Fiona's emerald eyes grew distant.

Ronan could only guess what she contemplated, but the white glow of her palms gave away her excitement.

Finally, she spoke again, her words tumbling out in a rush. "If what you say is true and there's a chance we can beat Emuirdane, finally defeat him once and for all . . ."

She held the flask aloft for them all to see. "Then this changes everything."

20

In the chill morning mists, the forest was quiet, tranquil and calm under dawn's first blush.

And just as silent was the man standing still, his amber eyes scanning the woods.

Fiona stood well behind him, musing over the object he held in his hand. Ronan, it seemed, had harbored one final secret—the clay disc that sat in his palm. Molded from the mud of Mount Aeylwon, it had been created by the goddess herself.

The artifact allowed Ronan to detect the Ceffyl's general location. And once the animal drew close enough, she'd be summoned to Ronan when he broke the seal.

It was clear why he'd kept the relic a secret, despite their newfound alliance. How could he be sure Fiona wouldn't use it, or otherwise give it to Emuirdane to track the horse himself? Trust between them was fluid that way. And truth be told, she couldn't blame him.

Because she still harbored a secret of her own.

With that weighing on her mind, Fiona faced her mother. "Should we have brought Jack and Brit with us? What if we need more help? What if—"

"Fiona." Like her eyes, Nadia's voice was steady and calm. "We made the right decision leaving them with your grandfather. Emuirdane can be tricky, and . . ." Now she paused, as if carefully selecting her words.

"However you choose to handle this situation, it's best that we're all prepared. Whatever *your decision*," she emphasized the words, making sure Fiona understood the choice was hers and Ronan's to make, "we need to anticipate Emuirdane's anger and be ready for his every move, every possible strike he could make against our family."

Fiona nodded. "You're right. You're right. That's why I called Kat and told her to go to the house. If there's the smallest chance Emuirdane would retaliate against her . . ." She blew out a breath and shuddered.

"Listen to me." Her mother hooked an arm through Fiona's, pressing their cheeks together briefly. "For once, you have got to stop worrying about the rest of us. The Dea Matrona trusted you with the Ceffyl's fate. You and Ronan. And I may be biased, but as far as warriors go, I believe destiny chose pretty well."

"A warrior and a *witch*." Fiona laughed lightly.

"I didn't misspeak," Nadia said. "I meant *warriors*. Because you are one too." She turned to Fiona and cupped her face with both hands. "You worry, you second guess, but not because of self-doubt. It's because you care about other people. You take their pain into yourself."

Emotion welled up inside of Fiona and crowded her throat. She couldn't speak past the feelings her mother roused, so she only stared into her velvety brown eyes.

"Your heart is tender. Sometimes too sensitive." She tapped Fiona's chest. "But that does not mean you're weak. That, my darling daughter, is your *greatest strength*."

Fiona bit down on her lip and embraced her mother.

"I needed to hear that," she whispered, still allowing her mother to hold her. She was overwhelmed by the task she'd been given. And the magnitude of the choice she'd already made.

"Granddad, Brit, your sisters," Nadia squeezed her again, "we all want you to know that we have faith. In you and in Ronan. The two of you are more alike than you think."

Fiona stepped back, swiping at a few runaway tears. "We are?" She wrinkled her nose. "I hope that's true, because—"

It was then Ronan lifted a hand and called to Fiona. "She's close." He beckoned her over as Nadia, Tate, and Sami spread out to form a semi-circle. Each had some of Ronan's orbs, filled with the shining black substance generated from Emuirdane's dark, dark magick.

Like her mother had said, they wanted to be ready for anything.

Fiona strode to stand with Ronan, her heart beating with such force she felt she might explode. Of all the options she'd considered since his arrival in her life, what she was about to do now had never been a consideration.

Not until lately, when piece-by-piece, the fragments slid into place, creating a vision of what must occur. Of what she must do.

Ronan's golden-brown gaze fastened on hers. "Are you ready?"

Dragging in a breath, Fiona inclined her head. "I am."

"I know you'll do the right thing, Fiona."

I hope so.

With his eyes still on hers, Ronan snapped the clay seal in two.

The quake in the ground was sudden yet mild, as he released the goddess's power. A few birds took flight, launching from the branch of a pine, as if they too had felt the tremor.

For several beats, they stood in the mist—pulses thrumming with growing tension—as they waited for the telltale sound of hooves.

So when the white horse eased quietly from the trees, her arrival drew gasps of awe. She sliced through the fog, head held high with regal grace.

When those gentle brown eyes looked to Fiona, certainty flooded in. "Jewel," she whispered. "You're as gorgeous as I remembered."

The horse tossed her head lightly, as if she both heard and agreed, and Fiona couldn't help but smile.

"The bundle," Ronan said, indicating the gemstones still wrapped in corduroy, set nearby on a large flat stone.

Hands shaking, Fiona retrieved the roll and returned to his side.

With a slow, easy gait, the Ceffyl walked to them, having answered the call she could not refuse. The fate she could only obey.

"Both of us should place the gems on the Ceffyl." Ronan's voice was low and somber, as suited the occasion. "Fiona," he said when she didn't respond.

Clasping the bundle in her hands, Fiona looked to the pristine white mare standing before them. She thought again of the Dea Matrona's words.

Strength. Intuition. Heart.

Her heart, she realized, guided her decision. And her intuition told her it was right.

And her strength ... Well, she would need that most of all.

"Ronan," she said, "I hope you understand."

His brow furrowed with confusion. "Understand what, Fiona?" His eyes dropped to the roll and the gems it contained. "What are you doing?"

"I was the last person to possess the Jeweled Ceffyl." She forced herself to hold his intense stare.

"I don't see what that—" He broke off when comprehension struck. "Wait," he said, his arms out as he pled. "Fiona, don't."

She pressed one palm against the horse. "I'm sorry, Ronan, but I've made my decision." And drew a deep breath. "I'm taking my wish."

❀❀❀

The door slammed open and footsteps slapped across the tiles. "My lady!"

Veloria's voice rang with panic, and Hellana jerked upright in her bed. She sat, stunned, as the elderly healer moved with agility belying her age.

"We must go now. There is little time." Veloria's strained expression spoke of fear. Rushing to the bedside, she pulled a key from her apron and began unlocking Hellana's manacles.

"How do you already have the key? I thought you were to—"

"The plans have changed, my lady. I'm afraid I resorted to violence. I couldn't wait for a sleeping tonic to work on the sentinel guarding your husband's study. So I bashed him on the head."

"Veloria! The castle guard will be upon us when they find him, or if he wakes to report what happened."

"We will not be here by that time." Veloria freed Hellana's wrists and ankles, then she paused long enough to join hands with her mistress. "My lady." She swallowed and stared hard at Hellana. Then she softened. "My dove, we must go now. My sister has had a vision."

"Ayleen?" Hellana slipped into the sturdy boots Veloria had brought from the closet. "What has she seen? Why must we flee?" She glanced out the window. "And when the sun is still high? Surely we'll be discovered."

"We leave through the dungeon. A secret tunnel." Veloria firmed her lips. "The way is rough, dark, and wet. But there is no alternative. We leave. Now."

When the healer hurriedly wrapped Hellana up in a coat, the first real tentacles of fear worked their way inside. They coiled around her heart and wound into her gut, filling her with a cold and oily sense of dread.

"What is this about, Veloria?" She latched onto the older woman's arms. "Tell me of Ayleen's vision. Tell me what she's seen."

"Oh, my dove." Veloria's voice broke. "Something terrible is going to happen."

❈❈❈

Fiona touched the Jeweled Ceffyl to claim her wish. And a deep, dark chasm opened within Ronan. "You can't do this, Fiona. Every wish comes with a cost. The price is too high!"

Green eyes damp with unshed tears, she gazed steadily back at him. "It is a price I will gladly pay. To fulfill our destiny."

"I don't understand." If he'd been able, Ronan would have pulled her away from the horse, but even that would do no good. She'd already stated her intent. Nothing and no one could prevent the Ceffyl from giving her what she asked for now.

A jagged shard ripped through his chest, a physical pain that mirrored the depth of her betrayal. How could she do this? And why? What would she ask of the Ceffyl? Wealth? More power? Love? She had all of that.

"If this is about Emuirdane, I told you we can fight him. The weapons will work. He can't hurt you anymore." Ronan curled his hands into fists. "I won't let him hurt you!"

"Oh, Ronan. You're a good man, a born defender of those in need." A tear rolled down Fiona's cheek. "But this isn't about fear. Emuirdane's threats will no longer drive my life or direct my actions."

She stroked a hand down the horse's sleek neck. "This is about responsibility and doing what I know is right. I'm risking everything, not because I need something in return." Her sweet smile broke Ronan's heart. "But because my conscience tells me I must."

With that, she looked to the Ceffyl and continued her gentle caress. "I ask for my wish to be granted."

"Please, Fiona. Don't do this," Ronan begged. "Whatever you want, it's not worth it."

She ignored him, and when her soft voice rose into the air, Ronan knew she not only spoke to Jewel. But to the heavens, the goddess, and Fate itself. "I claim my right, here and now, as the last in possession of the Ceffyl. Let my wish be answered."

Fiona closed her eyes and put both hands on the horse's side. "I wish for the Jeweled Ceffyl to remain in animal form and never grant another wish."

Ronan went utterly still, unable to believe the words he'd heard. Shocked and humbled, he watched as the finest shimmer rose from the Ceffyl to disperse and fall like a thousand tiny diamonds.

Jewel shook her head and stomped her front feet before rearing up on hind legs. And when she neighed, it echoed through the forest, with a sound that could only be described as joy.

The joy of *freedom*.

As if on cue, a sunbeam cut through the trees, falling across the horse's pure white body.

Dropping her forelegs, Jewel returned to the ground and turned to nuzzle Fiona's outstretched hand. Then the animal cast her soft eyes toward Ronan.

And lowered to one knee.

Fiona beamed. "I think she's saying thank you."

"Why?" Ronan could barely speak. Wonder and amazement battled against doubt and uncertainty. How had he been blind to the answer Fiona had seen so clearly? "You're the one who set her free."

Jewel stood again when Fiona came to Ronan's side. "But you're the one who's protected her, kept her safe." Fiona touched his face. "You've devoted your entire life to guarding her. And that's something to be proud of."

Shaking his head, Ronan reached out to pet Jewel. "I couldn't see what had to be done." He turned his attention to Fiona. "But *you* did. And I should never have doubted you."

A shy smile curved her lips. "All that matters is that Jewel is safe. And whatever comes, you and I will face it together. We're stronger when united, Ronan."

"That we are." Swamped by the admiration he felt for this woman, Ronan ran his palms down her arms and took her hands.

"So the Ceffyl is free. Forever."

He leaned in to kiss her, but a foul wind tore through the trees, driving them apart. The stench of sulfur rode on its waves, while above them the clouds darkened, rolling across the sky as if driven by vengeance.

"Fiona!" Ronan reached out, made a grab for her hand. "Stay close to me!"

The environment grew suddenly heavy, as if the air held extra weight. And a silver haze rushed from the forest shadows, surging across the terrain with unnatural speed.

"He's here!" Tate shouted. "Emuirdane is here!"

"And he's *pissed*," Sami added, her legs braced against the gale and two orbs already in her hands.

Jewel reared again, but this time in terror. The horse bolted into the woods and was lost behind the dense veil of silver.

Ronan reached to his back and grasped his seelion, grateful for the new tips of gold. A late-night modification, compliments of Nadia and Sami.

When the Iele emerged from the mist, Ronan wondered if their weapons would be enough.

Emuirdane's face had morphed with rage, his cheeks elongated with dark hollows etched beneath his eyes. He roared like thunder and his lightning cracked. "Whiteburn!"

With heavy steps, the Iele advanced, his malicious stare centered on Fiona. As the wind gusted, he jabbed a long, clawed finger. "You," he snarled at her, each word spitting with hate. "What have you done?"

21

Darkness moved in and swallowed the forest, blinking out the new day to deliver them into hellish night. Across the ground, Emuirdane glided, racing in on an invisible tide.

With both arms raised, he bellowed his wrath. "You have ruined everything! Everything!" With a vicious spin he shoved out his magick, bringing the monstrous trees around them to life. Limbs and branches became arms and legs, while gaping mouths opened wide in the trunks.

Horror slammed into Fiona, crushed the air from her lungs. But she found her breath as the world went insane, as firs and pines pulled their roots free to walk. "It's a glamour!" she screamed to her mother and sisters. "It's only a glamour!"

Too late, she saw the branch swing down, cutting through the air with a whistle. The quick lash sliced through her cheek, and pain erupted.

"Fiona!" Ronan yelled from somewhere behind her. And in the next instant, another object whizzed past her head.

She ducked and whooshed out a gasp, still reeling from the blow to her face and the warmth of blood gushing down her neck.

But the flying object flashed bright in the dark, and Emuirdane howled when the blade cleaved into his arm. A green bolt split the air, lighting the ground with a short burst of green. "Gold!" he yelled, focused on Ronan. "How dare you, Legion filth! I should have melted your bones the last time, but your whore begged for your life."

Electricity began to build in the Iele's hands. "I won't make that mistake again."

Emuirdane loosed a scorching strike, but Ronan dove to the side, rolling in an evasive maneuver.

Fiona took advantage of Emuirdane's distraction. "Sami, the orbs! Use them now!"

Sami didn't waver but hurled one of the glass balls at Emuirdane's back. The globe shattered and released its power, the glittering particles adhering to the Iele's body. Face, hands, clothing—he was covered in black dust.

He whipped and turned, cursing in a language Fiona didn't understand. Then he pivoted and zeroed in on Sami. "I'll rip out your eyes and rape your bloody skull, just as I wanted to the first night I saw you. The night on the cliffs. Remember, Sami?"

Emuirdane's tone was serpentine as he undulated his fingers. "Don't you know I lusted for you from the start?" He tossed an invisible spell. "Feel my love now!"

Sami screamed and slapped her hands to her face. "My eyes! My eyes!"

"No!" Fiona reached for her own power and leveled it at Emuirdane. Her magick punched into his body, buckling his knees and shoving him off balance.

When he stabilized, he whirled around and took stalking strides toward Fiona. Nadia and Tate closed in from the side, and flung two more orbs, both hitting at the same time.

He swatted the air as if being stung by wasps. "Vile, mortal bitches!" Eyes burning green, Emuirdane bucked and heaved.

But he was still on his feet. And still coming for Fiona.

He retracted his arms, then threw them out.

She summoned air to create a shield, bracing for the impact. Her mother screamed. Ronan lunged.

Fiona tensed . . . but nothing happened.

For a moment Emuirdane froze, as if unsure what he had done. He flicked his wrists again, but like before, no lightning formed.

Sami had fallen to her knees under the Iele's assault, but now she stood, lowering her hands from her face.

"Are you okay?" Tate ran to Sami, patting her cheeks and inspecting her eyes.

Sami nodded.

Fiona smoothed fingers over her own face, but the wound and blood were gone.

Without his magick, Emuirdane's glamours weakened and died. The winds calmed, the black sky cleared, and one by one, monsters turned back into trees.

"What torment is this?" Emuirdane stretched out an arm to stare at the black sparkles clinging to his skin. Slowly the green faded from his eyes. "What have you done to me?"

"No more than you deserve." Fiona circled the evil Fae who'd wreaked havoc on her life for far too long. "We can fight you, Emuirdane. Because we have your magick. We know its secrets."

Standing tall, she stared him down. "We can defeat your power." Her voice rang true and clear. "And we can defeat *you*."

"Impossible. No human could—" He broke off and sent a baleful look to Ronan. "You helped them do this. You and your Legion."

Fiona spoke harshly, trying to keep his attention on her. "The Ceffyl can no longer give you what you want. There is no more artifact. There is nothing for you here." Taking two strides toward him, she raised her palms, let her fire flame bright. "Never return to our world, Emuirdane. Never threaten or harass any of us again."

"I will drag you to my dungeons and—"

"No," Tate cut in. "You won't."

"We stand together on this." Nadia approached him, brandishing a shining globe.

"Your father owes me!" Emuirdane shrieked at her. "*You* owe me. You'd be dead if I hadn't saved you." He threw out his hand, but still no magick.

"And we have paid," Nadia continued. "In suffering and loss, fear and pain. We have paid you and Hellana more than you were ever owed."

"So go," Ronan said, his brown eyes stern, his posture unyielding. "Let this family be at peace. The Jeweled Ceffyl is no more, liberated with the blessing of the Dea Matrona."

"The goddess," Emuirdane said with a sneer. "That interfering—"

Sami advanced on the dark Fae, waving the seelion she'd retrieved from the ground. "And in case you think of returning, I'll be sure to make more of these." With a flourish, she displayed the golden blades. Poison to the Iele.

When Emuirdane blocked his face with a shaking arm, Sami laughed and handed the weapon back to Ronan.

Emuirdane huffed. And huffed again, as if his arrogant mind couldn't grasp this new hierarchy where he ruled no more. "This isn't over," he said with a snarl. But his attempt to intimidate had lost its edge.

Turning his gaze away to the forest, he whirled his black cloak and conjured silver mists. But before he vanished, he spoke to Fiona. "Take care, witch, for the next time we meet—"

"One of us will die," she said, beating him to the threat.

As the mists enfolded him, Emuirdane vanished.

They watched him go, and released a collective sigh.

"To tell the truth," Fiona's mother said, "I was worried he wouldn't be able to leave. It's his magick that allows him to travel between realms."

Fiona hadn't considered that possibility, but cringed at the thought of Emuirdane being stuck in her world.

"The orbs and their enchantment trap his powers within, so he can't send it out." Ronan edged up to Fiona's side. "But transporting is an internal magick."

"I'm just glad he's gone, and that it's finally over." Sami put her hands on her hips, darted her eyes to the others. "It *is* over, right? I mean, this feels like a victory."

Fiona's mother nodded, taking Sami and Tate in her arms. "I don't think he'll be back. Something inside tells me he won't be back." Her bright smile broke through. "I believe Emuirdane is gone for good."

Tate exhaled heavily. "I can't believe it could really be true. We've dreaded Emuirdane and his sadistic ways for so long. We've gone through so much." Her arm still around Sami and their mother, Tate sent a tender smile to Fiona. "Today's confrontation happened so fast. It almost seems too easy."

With a glance to Ronan, Fiona sighed. "None of this has been easy."

Tate was nodding in understanding when a soft whinny carried on the breeze.

As one, they all turned their attention to the woods. And watched as Jewel trotted slowly through the pines. The horse came to stand before Fiona and Ronan, as trustingly as she had before.

"Looks like she wants to go home with you," Sami teased.

Fiona met Jewel's sweet brown gaze. "Actually," she said, glancing aside to Ronan, "I have a better idea."

His crooked grin turned up at one corner before reaching his eyes. He gave a single nod.

Fiona looked to Tate. "Will you call Jack and Brit? Ask them to bring the trailer?" Leaning into Ronan, she took him by the hand. "We've got one more thing we need to do."

Mr. Walsh wore a bemused expression when he stepped out onto his porch, the old brown hat hanging in his hand. But when Ronan and Fiona got out of the car, the man's mask of confusion turned to bitterness. "You two could have called, and I'd have saved you the trip. I haven't seen the horse."

Still on the top step, he whacked his hat against his leg. Behind him, the door opened again as Tyler strode out.

"We've come to make you an offer," Ronan called out, skirting the SUV and the trailer it hauled.

Mr. Walsh frowned. "Whatever it is, I'm not buying. Especially from you two."

"Mr. Walsh." Fiona stepped forward, her hands out in supplication. "Please hear us out. What happened before . . ." She paused and bit her lip. "Well, it's a long and complicated story. But we, Ronan and I," she gestured to where he was hidden behind the vehicle, "we wanted to tell you how sorry we are about what happened. And I promise you—we never, and *would* never, hurt an innocent animal."

Mr. Walsh continued to glare while Tyler crossed his arms over his chest.

But both of their faces relaxed into lines of surprise when Ronan walked into view with Jewel.

"You found her," Tyler said, just as Mr. Walsh hurried down the steps to greet the horse.

"There's a sweet girl," the older man crooned, rubbing her neck and down along her flank. "Aren't you a beautiful sight? Just the most beautiful sight."

The way he gushed over the mare told Fiona they'd made the right call. She and Ronan shared a quick smile.

Jewel nuzzled Mr. Walsh's hands and gave a low nicker of pleasure.

"Ms. Whiteburn and I have come to an agreement." Ronan released Jewel's rein to Mr. Walsh.

"What kind of agreement?" Tyler asked. Unlike his uncle, he was clearly still suspicious.

With a wave of his hand, Ronan deferred to Fiona.

"We need to find Jewel a good home," she said. "We thought

we knew where she would be going." Fiona sidled closer to Ronan, gave a small chuckle. "But as it turns out, we were both wrong."

Mr. Walsh looked up, his eyes brimming with curiosity . . . and a bit of hope.

"A loving home," she added, moving to stand near the man and the horse he adored. "Would you be interested in having her back, Mr. Walsh?"

"I would." His head bobbed quickly. "But how much—"

"Free," Ronan said. "No charge at all." He pulled Jewel's registration papers from inside his coat and offered them to Tyler who'd walked down to join them. "All we ask is that you love her, care for her, and let her live a long, happy life."

A loud neigh made them all turn toward the paddock at the end of the stables. Fiona laughed. "It looks like Dante's happy to see her again too."

"We all are. Indeed we are." Unabashedly, Mr. Walsh wiped his teary eyes. "I can't tell you how much this means. I don't know why, but I grew attached to her so quickly." He caressed Jewel's nose and received an appreciative snuffle in response.

Fiona's heart sighed one time and her own eyes burned. "She's a very special horse."

Ronan came up behind her, put his hands on her shoulders. "She most definitely is."

"I'll just go get her settled in then," Mr. Walsh said. "And thank you," he told them both, extending a hand in gratitude. "You've made an old man happy today."

"Tyler," Fiona said when the man made as if to follow his uncle. "If you can use the trailer, it's yours as well."

Tyler lifted his brows. "Fiona, that's quite an expensive gift."

"Call it payment for the room and board you gave Jewel this winter."

Tyler shook his head and clucked his tongue. "Like I said before," he smiled and hooked a thumb to his departing uncle, "that's between you and the boss."

"Need any help?" Ronan asked as Tyler headed to the hitch.

"Not at all, but thanks. Just give me a minute or two."

Fiona leaned back against Ronan's chest, watching as Jewel and Dante sniffed noses across the paddock fence.

Ronan wrapped his arms around her, enjoying the pretty picture the two animals made, her gleaming white and his midnight black. For a moment they stood in the crisp, cool wind, both saying their silent goodbyes to a horse known only as Jewel.

22

The mood inside the car was solemn, especially considering the triumph of the day. Emuirdane had been beaten, and Jewel was free.

Yet Fiona sat beside Ronan, gripping her hands in her lap.

They rode in silence until the outskirts of Bar Harbor, when she finally gave life to the questions on her mind. "What will you do now?" She kept her gaze straight ahead, her eyes on the road. "Will you return to Faerie?"

Ronan couldn't lie, not to her. And he wouldn't evade, as that was tantamount to the same thing. "I will," he said gently. "The Legion, the council—they all will have questions. Despite what's happened, I still have an obligation as their commander. I have to lead the men through the transition, whatever that may turn out to be."

She glanced aside, sent him a tentative smile. "I wouldn't expect any less of you." She shifted in her seat, curled her fingers to her palms. "And this transition, it might take a while."

It wasn't a question, but with no way to say otherwise, Ronan could only nod.

When she looked at him this time, her gaze was steady. "Then I don't want to go back home." She drew a soft breath. "I'd rather go to your room at the inn. This may be your last night here."

The first heavy drops of rain splattered on the windshield.

"And I want us to spend it together."

Moved beyond words, Ronan took her hand. Lifted it and kissed her fingers. "Are you sure?" he asked, keeping the contact between them.

Her lips turned up sweetly, with just a hint of the wicked. "I'm absolutely sure."

The gleam in her green eyes was all the motivation he needed. At the intersection he made a quick stop, then a hard left toward the heart of town.

By the time they reached the inn, the sky had opened up. Ronan started around to Fiona's door, but she was already out and sprinting through the rain. In the air, her laughter trailed, like a woodland nymph on the run.

Ronan's blood fired, and he found himself giving chase. More than ready to play the game. "You can't get in without the key!"

"Ha!" she called back, slowing to take the curve near the fountain and up the steps. "I have my ways."

Ronan hurried after her, jerking open the doors. But he slowed to a respectable pace when he saw the woman with towels in her arms. He sent a wave as he passed her by. "Good day, Angie."

Her eyes darted down the hall after Fiona. "For some of us it is." Then she gave him a wink.

Deciding the comment was best left unanswered, he rounded the corner in time to see Fiona slip into his room. Witches and their tricks, he thought with a grin.

And couldn't wait to see a few more.

When he got to the room he eased inside, to a space banked in stormy-day shadows. He closed the door while his eyes adjusted.

"Can't see in the dark, warrior?" Fiona's voice came from his left.

He could make out her shape against the window, dark curves in silhouette. His heart sped up faster now than when he'd been running. "You're in a playful mood."

"I am," she said, barely audible over the driving rain. "Because I've learned something today."

Ronan moved closer and took in the sight of her. Her black hair was drenched, as were her clothes. They clung to her body with erotic suggestion.

"What have you learned?" He rounded the end of the bed, cornering her between it and the wall.

She danced her fingertips—just the tips—up his arm. "To follow my heart, to listen to my instincts." She stepped into him. "And do you know what they're telling me now?"

She put her fingers to his lips, hushing his reply. "That you're the man I was meant to love." Her lips brushed his before she whispered against them, "If only for this one night."

Ronan's heart simply stumbled and fell.

"You've become a fire within me." He pressed her palm to the center of his chest. "Right here. Bringing light to places I never knew were in shadow." His breath shuddered out of him. "I can't go back to the darkness, Fiona."

She trembled against him. "But you have to leave."

He dropped his forehead to hers. "Then love me now." The words were a plea. "Love me enough to last forever."

Her emerald eyes deepened with desire, and she pulled him forward, her mouth capturing his in a slow, seductive rhythm. She leaned into the kiss, and then retreated. And grasping his hips, she lowered her face.

To lick a single drop of rain from his chest.

The gesture drew a moan from Ronan. He'd expected the sweet—but not the bold.

He popped her top button, then teased her shirt apart. Felt a shock of lust to find her bare underneath. Inch by painstaking inch, he exposed her creamy skin, trailing one finger through the valley of her breasts.

She arched her body and parted her lips, letting her head fall back to expose her neck.

Ronan tasted her there. And it was all he could take.

In one quick move, he ripped off his shirt. Another and they were on the bed—hot, slick, and wrapped up in each other.

"I'll never look at the rain the same way again." He raked his teeth over her damp shoulder.

And was rewarded when her hips shot up to meet his.

He ached to go slowly, to memorize every dip and curve, taste all her secret places. But they were riding the dragon now, with nothing to do but hold on tight.

The rest of their clothes couldn't come off fast enough. But once they did, his eyes raked over her, his gaze a whisper touch on her soft flesh. Unable to resist, he lowered himself back down, his body molding to hers.

He heard her sigh, then whimper with desire.

The heat between them was unimaginable. Scorching. Scalding. Like embracing the sun.

And here with her, loving her this way, he could finally admit his own driving need. That need was to have Fiona. To have her in his life.

"You're beautiful, compassionate, and so very brave. Now I know you. Now I see you." He cupped her face and kissed her lips. "Exactly as you are."

Something snapped inside Fiona, filling her heart with a long, lovely sigh. "And I see you," she breathed, reveling in the truth of Ronan's words. The barriers once between them now had crumbled, leaving no more secrets. No more deceit.

She sensed his nod in the dark, just before his mouth found hers again. She'd imagined this moment, but wasn't prepared. She'd never expected the depth of his love.

Just like finding her magick, he had been a surprise, an intoxicating and powerful rush in her blood. But even the thrilling sensation of her abilities paled in comparison to the gift he gave.

As if he knew her thoughts, and that the time had come, Ronan's hands slipped along the arch of her back, holding her tight as he settled between her thighs.

Anticipation curled inside her, a hot twisting spring, as the need to have him clawed for release. "Ronan," she sunk her hands into his deep brown hair. "I have to feel you inside me. That final connection."

He stilled against her and whispered of his love, claiming her heart with those golden eyes. As he pushed inside and claimed her body.

His need—his possession—was unapologetic, and her body responded with a long, liquid pull. She wanted to watch, to stay lost in his eyes, but pleasure took over when he moved his hips.

One full, deep stroke, and she thought she'd go mad. Then he drove deeper, and she started to spin. Ecstasy and emotion swirled into one, lifting her high on that marvelous crest.

And this time when his name found her lips, it rose atop the sweet sound of passion. The sound of love.

And in that moment, the sound of forever.

❊❊❊

In another dark room, in another realm, Emuirdane materialized in a cloud of mist. Fury still rode his back, flogging him through space and time. For even now as he stood in his study, the horrid black specks adhered to his skin.

He opened the decanter atop his desk, and poured himself far too much wine. His flesh had begun to throb and burn, from his own magick trapped inside his skin.

Damn that Legion bastard! He and the witch had ruined it all. And with only a few short hours until the Stag Moon rose.

He had no Ceffyl to give King Malrik, and he would see the

flames of Hadon before he'd give up his blood.

Despair was an unknown discomfort, its misery an ache he was eager to shed. Hoping to numb that pain, he downed the drink in one long gulp. And when his wrath reared up again, he smashed the empty glass against the door.

Immediately, a sentinel rushed in. "My lord, there is news—"

"Bring me the healer," Emuirdane barked.

The guard paused, his face drawn and pale.

Curling his upper lip, Emuirdane grabbed a second glass and slammed it on the desk. His voice was like gravel, grating in his throat. "A healer now or it's to the dungeons. Your choice."

The white-faced man lurched into action, tripping over his own feet and bumping into the door. "Right away, my lord." He all but flew from the room.

Emuirdane ripped off his cape and rolled up his sleeves. With narrowed eyes, he studied his hands. At last, it seemed, the glisten was fading, and soon his power would be restored.

But to what end? What would become of him when the Stag Moon reached its pinnacle?

Low voices and hurried steps carried from the hall, jolting him from his ruminations, before two guards entered the study. Between them, they held a young girl with hair the color of wheat.

This time Emuirdane flung the entire decanter. Glass exploded on the wall panel near the guard's face, and crimson rivulets drained to the floor. "Why am I surrounded by imbeciles? I need the healer. Now!"

"Sh-sh-she *is* a healer, my lord." The guard stuttered and shrank into himself.

Emuirdane ground his teeth. He bared his fangs. "Fools! I want Veloria. The royal healer."

The two men exchanged a wary glance. "She's gone, my lord. That is what I tried to report."

"Gone? She can't be gone. She wouldn't dare leave without my consent." Emuirdane pounded the desk with both fists. "She is needed here, to care for my wife!"

The same guard took a slight step in retreat. From across the room, Emuirdane saw the man's throat bob with fear. "She has gone as well. We believe the two absconded together. M-my lord. Sir."

Emuirdane couldn't think. He couldn't move. Shock and denial were poison in his veins.

"What say you?" he asked, his tone deceptively soft, as he stared over the guards' heads and into thin air.

"Queen Hellana has fled with the healer called Veloria. The old woman struck me down. She stole your keys to the—"

"Silence." The whispered word echoed through the chamber. "You're saying she has escaped me? Again?"

The man looked as if he might pass out.

Shifting his glower to the second guard, Emuirdane pointed to the first. "Arrest him and put him in chains. I'll have no man in my guard who would fall beneath the hands of a weak old woman."

"My lord." The second guard inclined his head and called for more men. The newcomers arrested the gaping first guard, bundling him away and off to the gaol.

"And I need more wine!" he yelled at the guards who remained. He needed buckets of wine to drown such betrayal.

His lovely Hellana had left him again.

Then his mind snapped from despair to revenge. "That ungrateful whore."

She'd simpered and mewled, playing the role of dutiful wife, all the while plotting yet another escape. Well, he was done being gentle. No longer would she receive a queen's treatment.

Rage blackened his vision and drummed in his brain. She would know true pain by the end of this night!

"Call up three men from the vanguard, and bring me a new set of clothing!" Spying the girl still huddled near the door, Emuirdane growled, "And you. Bring me a draught to boost my strength."

If his magick remained weak, at least his body would not.

"Aye, sir." She bobbed in a curtsy and sped away.

Like an animal, his wife had crawled away. And like an animal, he would track her down.

With the idea fresh in his mind, he caught the eye of the last guard. "Wake the kennel master, and loose the hounds." He would use the creatures Hellana loved to sniff her out. He would let the beasts have the old woman for a meal. Devour the hag in front of his wife.

Not only had Hellana left her husband by law, but she had also stolen his unborn child. The Draviski heir and Emuirdane's own—

Everything around him went silent as death, as a terrible yet wonderful solution emerged.

"Wait!" he called after the last man. Tearing off his ruined garments, he ran for the door. "I want everything brought to the gates. Including my horse."

In the hallway he paused to stare through a window and farther beyond to the indigo sky. Where two shining moons had yet to meet.

"Tonight I join the hunt."

23

The next day dawned bright and clear, as if the yellow sun were announcing the spring.

And Ronan felt just as optimistic when he and Fiona entered the kitchen of her home.

This might be his last day in the mortal world, at least for a while. But he maintained the hope that things had truly changed, and that the Ceffyl's liberation might mean freedom for him as well.

Not that he'd ever viewed his position in the Legion as a hardship. He never had. But now that he'd found Fiona, the idea of a regular life held brand new appeal.

Even if that life included Sami who, it seemed, never missed out on an opportunity to tease.

"Well, well. Look what the cat dragged in." Leaning against the counter, glass of water in her hand, Sami sent the two newcomers a smug yet playful grin. "You *did* just come home, right, Fee?"

"Yep," Fiona replied smartly, leaning up to give Ronan a smack on the lips. "Jealous much, sis?"

"Ouch." Sami waved her hand as if she'd been stung. "What have you done to our mild-mannered Fiona?"

"I'm afraid I haven't met this person," Ronan said, then dodged when Fiona punched lightly for his arm.

Sami lifted one shoulder and sipped her drink, but over the rim of her glass she sent him a smile.

As if on cue, the side door opened to admit Tate and Jack. "Greetings, mortals," Tate chimed out, apparently feeling quite cheerful herself. But then, the absence of one immortal Fae probably had quite a lot to do with that.

The only ones missing were Fiona's grandfather and Brit.

"Breakfast, Ronan?" Nadia was scrambling eggs on the stove. "We've got cinnamon buns in the oven, though I'm afraid mine aren't as good as Fiona's."

"Mom." Fiona crossed over and put her head to Nadia's. "Whose recipe do you think I use?"

A general sense of familial accord fell over the scene and, Ronan was pleased to note, he seemed to be included. Jack joined him before the fireplace, though no flames jumped on this pleasant day. Together they watched the four women chat, laugh, and buzz around like bees.

Tate carried over two plates, each loaded down with eggs, bacon, and a fat, frosted cinnamon bun. "Coffee, Ronan?" she asked with a smile, as if their trouble in Faerie had never happened.

"Please," he said. "I take it black."

The atmosphere remained cordial and lively, with each family member fighting to tell him stories of Fiona. Each one endeared her to him, and he put his hand on her leg beneath the table, trying to convey how much her family's acceptance meant to him.

And he would have stayed there until the end of the day. If not for the golden light emanating from a corner of the room.

"Oh, no," Sami said, spotting the glow. She set her dishes in the sink with a clunk. "Here we go again."

Ronan moved from the table and stood at attention, the gesture of respect still ingrained.

The goddess's messenger had come with a missive, one detailing his return trip to Faerie. Back to his duty and his life far away.

Ronan had the urge to touch Fiona, to feel her near. But like a good soldier, he stood statue-still.

The brilliant light began to fade, and astonishment rolled through him like the tide. He bowed down to the unexpected visitor.

Not Rhiann.

But the goddess herself.

Her pale pink gown held unearthly luminescence, as did her silver hair and eyes.

"My lady," he said, his tone low in reverence.

Fiona went still and then lowered her head. Still gazing down, she tugged at her sister's elbow. Sami quickly mirrored her example. As did the others in the room.

"Please, be at ease." The Dea Matrona extended her hands. "For I have come with commendations. To offer my praise and my thanks." Her silvery eyes fell upon Ronan and Fiona. "To express nothing less than my eternal gratitude."

Pride streamed through Ronan's blood, like a line of light displacing all doubt. There was no question that the goddess was pleased. That she approved of Fiona's unselfish wish.

"It was an honor to serve you, my lady." He turned to Fiona. "But the credit is not mine."

"You both made the way clear," the goddess said. "And you could not have triumphed without one another." She floated across the floor, stopping before Ronan. "I know you have questions about your future, and that is also why I came. To deliver news." She tilted her head and beamed. "News I believe you will find most welcome."

Ronan drew a breath, held it inside.

"I expect you to return to Faerie and oversee the changes that must take place. Because the Legion shall be no more. The ranks shall disband."

"My lady?" Ronan asked. "What would you have us do?"

"Whatever you like, for you have earned that reward."

Fiona gasped and took Ronan's hand.

"I could not see the end that was to come." Including Fiona in her approving gaze, the Dea Matrona continued. "But now that it has, I know there was never any other. A wish to free the giver of wishes, a conclusion both poetic and just."

Ronan caught a glimpse of grief in the deity's eyes. "All has come full circle. From the salvation of one child . . ." She pressed her lips together and raised her chin. "I am happy to have brought this announcement myself, for you both have my highest regard. But now I shall depart."

"My lady," Ronan began, a sliver of unease pricking at his mind. "You referred to one child." He paused and again saw her silver eyes cloud over. "As if there is another?"

The Dea Matrona shook her head. "It is no concern of yours. You should rest now and be well."

"Forgive me, my lady, but what child?" Fiona asked. "I don't understand." She squeezed Ronan's hand, and he could see her recalling the goddess's words. "What did you mean? When you said it had all come full circle?"

With a fist to her stomach, Fiona pressed on. "You were talking about the original child. The child that was saved."

Ronan picked up the line of thought. "So it must follow that another is in danger." His conscience could not ignore the subject nor, he was certain, would the woman at his side. "What child, my lady? What else has transpired?"

"I did not want to burden your minds with such matters, as this is not your burden to bear. An oracle only just brought this development to my attention. But please know," she said earnestly, "none of this was seen before. This consequence was never predicted. As I told you once, the actions of individuals are not pre-determined."

"Please," Fiona said, her voice thick with fear. "I don't understand. What individuals?"

Nadia came to her daughter, lending what comfort she could.

Sami and Tate closed in as well.

"Emuirdane was in need of the Jeweled Ceffyl. He had promised the artifact to another, a contractual payment." The Dea Matrona smoothed the rosy fabric of her gown. "But he was given another option, a chance to settle the debt with blood. And now he plans to pay in full."

Ronan's body went cold through and through. "I can't imagine Emuirdane would give his own life."

"No. It is not his own blood he offers." Even the goddess shuddered. "But the innocent blood of his son."

❈❈❈

Fiona stood in a kind of trance, her body numb from the weight of guilt. She felt someone touch her shoulder, but she couldn't move in response. "A son? Emuirdane has a son?"

Silver eyes full of sorrow, the goddess gave a slight tip of her head. "He will soon, yes."

"Soon?" The meaning of her words was a sledgehammer to her chest. "You mean a *baby*? Emuirdane's son has yet to be born?"

"Oh, my God," Tate whispered, pressing her hand to her mouth. She leaned on Jack, horrified and stunned. As they all were.

But mostly Fiona, as this was the end she had wrought. She staggered abruptly, stumbled a step, engulfed and weakened by horror and shame.

But Ronan was there to catch her, to soothe her with his voice. "You didn't do this, Fiona. You couldn't have known."

Clinging to him for support, she looked to the goddess. "Emuirdane would sacrifice his newborn son?"

The Dea Matrona spread her hands. "It is his nature."

Fiona didn't cry. The shock went too deep for tears. But she let Ronan hold her as she drowned in remorse.

"I am sorry. I had hoped to keep this from you." The Dea

Matrona's expression held sadness and regret. "But again, I must tell you, no one knew. Not before today. And Fiona," the goddess said, "even the oracles of the gods did not anticipate this outcome, so you must not blame yourself."

"How can I not? My choices affected Emuirdane's." Like a row of vicious dominoes. "It doesn't matter that I didn't know."

Finding some of her strength, Fiona stood on her own. "What matters is that I know it now. And what matters," she said, her rage spreading like fire, "is what I decide to do about it."

"What can you do?" Sami asked. "We don't know anything about Emuirdane's world. Where it is, how to get there. And if we did, what then? He's a *king*, Fiona. And kings have armies."

"I don't think there's time to create more orbs." When her mother spoke, Fiona turned around. "You wouldn't be able to contain his magick." She looked past Fiona, met the goddess's stare. "How long do we have?"

Grateful for her mother's instant understanding, Fiona whirled and awaited the answer.

"Hours in his world. But less in yours."

"There's no time, Fee," Sami argued. "We don't know how to reach that realm, or if there's even a portal."

Disappointment returned, causing Fiona's shoulders to sag.

Until Ronan spoke. "My lady," he asked, "could you send us there?"

The Dea Matrona folded her hands together. "If it is what you wish. But the Ielonaar Realm is a treacherous place, and its night holds many dangers. Some worse than Emuirdane."

"What could possibly be worse?" Sami asked under her breath.

The goddess didn't answer.

"I have to go," Fiona said. She waved a hand when Sami began to protest. "I know you think I'm being too sensitive and that I'm putting the welfare of another before my own, but this is different, because a child is at risk. I cannot live with its death on my hands."

"I wasn't going to argue." Sami gave a casual shrug. "I can see when your mind is made up. I was just going to say I need two minutes." She glanced to the goddess. "Can I have that much time?"

"Why?" Fiona asked as Ronan moved to confer with Jack. "This can't wait."

"Because if you're going, then I'm going. But the daggers Mom made us are out in the shop." Sami's brown eyes held malicious intent. "Gold, remember? They're marbled with gold."

"Poison to the Iele. Yes," Fiona nodded with vigor. "We'll take all three."

"I'll handle my own, thank you." Tate crossed her arms over her chest. "And you know we have to call Brit. He won't want to be left behind."

"You don't have to do this." Fiona touched Ronan's face. "None of you do."

She placed a shaking hand on her stomach. "It's just that . . . it's a baby, even if an Iele, the child of our enemies. It's still an innocent." She shook her head and met Ronan's eyes. "Emuirdane is a king. No one will stand against him. And that little baby has no one else."

Taking her face between his palms, Ronan trapped her in his golden gaze. "He has us."

24

Hellana lost her footing on the rocky incline. "Veloria, I can't. I can't go any farther." She gripped the hard ball of her belly where the cramps had set in. All day they'd walked, taking only a brief rest in an abandoned hut.

Now they pushed on, in the dead of night, still too near the castle for any peace of mind.

"You can, my dove. You must go on." Though the healer's voice was full of encouragement, her tired and dirty face revealed her strain. "We have to make it as far as the river."

Night had fallen across the land, but the twin moons—those gods-damned moons—still lighted the way around the mountain pass.

A new burn ripped through Hellana's abdomen, the spasms in her back only doubling the pain. She stifled a scream, but dropped to her knees. "Please, please." Her words expelled on each panting breath. "I can hardly walk. My time is near."

"You must continue." Veloria's tone turned hard, as it did every time Hellana begged for respite. "You cannot birth your babe here. The drop is long and the trail unstable." The old woman sent a wary glance around the unforgiving terrain. "And too many creatures roam in the dark."

As if in answer, a lone howl rang out, its menacing bay resounding in the night.

"My gods. My gods. He's freed the hounds." Hellana forged

through the crippling agony and stood to walk. "And that sound means they've got our scent."

"Then we must make haste! We're almost to the other side, and then we'll be descending to the river." Veloria gave Hellana her shoulder to lean on. "Can you stay strong, my dove? Can you push a little farther?"

In the pale light of the two moons, the healer's face was stark white. "For if not, the beasts will be upon us too soon."

❋❋❋

The first thing Fiona noticed was the smell, like overturned earth with a hint of sulfur. "This place smells like Emuirdane's wrath." She wrinkled her nose but scanned the surroundings—craggy mountains, dense forest, and a rough gravel road before them.

"This is . . . picturesque," Sami observed with a heavy dose of sarcasm.

"But we must be close." Brit pulled the crossbow from his back and readied a bolt. "The Dea Matrona said she'd put us in Hellana's vicinity."

Like Sami and Fiona, Tate had her dagger on her belt, rigid steel with veins of swirling gold. She palmed the handle as she spoke. "And I wonder what sort of reception we'll get from her. Hellana did want us dead, and failing at that, she kept Mom as her prisoner."

Fiona shook off the chill racing down her back. The Ielonaar realm felt cold and perilous, foreign not only in landscape but in the strange bluish glow from the double moons above. "We stop Emuirdane and save the child. Then, if need be, we will deal with Hellana."

"So which way should we go?" Jack held his vellenium axe with both hands. There'd been no time to add gold to the weapon, but the enchanted metal would still deal some damage.

Ronan gestured up to the nearest mountain. "If I understood the goddess's instructions, Draviski Castle lies on the far side of those peaks." He returned his gaze to the road ahead, then held up a hand for silence. After a moment, he said, "I hear water."

"So do I." Sami motioned with the blade she was so eager to use. "That way."

"And that's where Hellana will go. She'll cross water, try to conceal her path in case she is followed." Ronan's expression was grim. "And we know that she will be."

Fiona spared a second to admire the man she'd fallen for, but then redirected her focus to the reason they were here. "I wonder if she's off of the mountain yet? We may be close, but with no idea which direction to go—"

She broke off when a woman's screams tore through the night.

"That way," Ronan said and began to run, along the road and toward the river.

Fiona and the others fell in with him, but she jolted when the voice came again. Only this in a terrified, "No! Please, no!"

"He's found her!" Fiona said, her legs pumping hard. When a chorus of howls overrode the screams, horror burst inside. Because Emuirdane wasn't the only monster trailing his wife.

❖❖❖

"Hellana, my darling." Emuirdane signaled the kennel master to call off the hounds. His wife was huddled beneath an overhanging rock, barely enough cover to protect her from rain. He tsked her like a child. "This is where you ran to? A hole in the ground to welcome my heir?"

"She's in labor, my lord," the healer cried out, one hand underneath Hellana's torn and filthy gown. "The head is crowning. Please, keep those beasts back!"

He'd brought three bloodhounds and three of the vanguard, just in case his plans went awry.

"Oh, I'll ensure the health of my child. Of that you can be certain." Emuirdane leaned down and slapped Veloria in the side of the head. "And I'll make sure you stay healthy too. At least until you are returned to my dungeons. I have such plans for you, old woman."

"Emuirdane," Hellana said and stopped to bear down.

"Don't speak," he warned his wife. "Don't beg. Or I'll rip out your tongue and feed it to the hounds. I'll hear no more of your lies, Hellana."

When she moaned and dropped back to the dirt, Emuirdane turned his ire to the healer again. "How much you suffer depends on how well you obey. Keep both my child and my wife alive. My need of your healing skills is all that is keeping you from becoming their dinner." He tossed a hand toward the massive bloodhounds, their skin, eyes, and mouths dripping thick crimson blood.

"Do you understand, Veloria?" He kneeled beside the old woman, lifted Hellana's dress for a peek. And instantly jumped to his feet. "Do you?" Appalled and disgusted by what he'd seen, he railed at the healer.

"Aye, my lord. I will keep them well." Her mouth trembled then twisted with hate. "And you, my lord? My *liege*," she added reproachfully. "Will you keep the babe safe? Will you see to the safety of your very own child?"

He drew back his fist, and was incredibly pleased to see his hand glowing green. His magick had returned. "Heed me, woman, and do your job. The dogs have yet to feed."

Behind him the hounds growled and snapped, and at last the healer showed true fear. She didn't speak but nodded quickly.

Hellana let loose an awful scream, then pulled herself up, latching onto her wide-spread knees. Her face turned red as she gritted her teeth, bearing down for what seemed like minutes.

At last her breath burst free and Veloria laughed. "There he is, my dove. You've got a fine, strapping boy." Laughing through tears, Hellana took the infant close to her breast.

Emuirdane looked on, but waited until the healer dealt with the cord and other . . . *revolting* substances.

Once the child was fully free, Emuirdane swooped in and snatched him up.

"Oh, wait, Emuirdane. Please, I beg of you." Hellana rolled to her knees, hands clasped as if in prayer. "Anything you want. Anything at all. Just don't hurt him." She sobbed loudly. "Don't give him to my father. You know what he will do!"

"Of course I know." Emuirdane's smile was mirthless and cruel. "That's why my plan will succeed."

"Don't," she gasped, throwing herself at him and grabbing onto his cloak.

He kicked her in the stomach.

Veloria gave a small cry and moved to help Hellana, but his wife was already crawling across the rocky ground. "Please, Emuirdane. Give him to me!"

He turned his back on the woman he cherished, and walked away with her tiny babe. "Take them to the castle," he told two of the soldiers. "I'll deal with them later."

As he strode away, Hellana grew hysterical. She screamed after him one final time, "No! Please, no!"

Before the baying of bloodhounds drowned out her pleas.

❊❊❊

"Quiet," Ronan said in a hushed tone, pointing to indicate he'd seen something up ahead. They'd followed the river around a bend, passing a trail that led up into the mountains. But whatever he'd seen was farther down the road, near an overhang of stone enshrouded by bushes.

With the moons so dazzling, there was no need for light. But when Fiona sensed a nearby threat, her palms burned a low, glowing white. "They're up there," she whispered, catching movement behind the shrubs.

And as soon as she'd spoken, a burly man in a uniform of dark green stepped into clear sight.

"How many?" Brit asked from behind. "Can you see?"

Ronan raised a hand and held one finger. Then he made it two. After observing a moment longer, he dropped his arm. "Only two as far as I can see. But there may be—"

"Nooo!" A wail shattered the stillness. "I'm not going back! I'm never going back!"

Fiona's heart went cold and then began to race.

"I have to stay here. He'll come back. I know he will. He has to come back!"

A second soldier emerged from behind the greenery, and with him he dragged a screaming, fighting Hellana. Her white gown was tattered and soiled, with stains of dirt—Fiona loosed a jagged breath—and red streaks of blood.

"She's had the baby," Ronan said, having come to the same conclusion as Fiona. "But I don't see Emuirdane."

"He's taken the baby." This from Sami who walked forward in a crouch, trying to keep from being spotted. "So what do we do?"

"We wait and see what and who we're dealing with." Brit's eyes locked on the two men and Hellana.

"There's another woman." Fiona spied an older female, following Hellana, it seemed, and apparently of her own free will.

The group of four walked across the ground and turned once they got to the road.

"They're heading this way," Jack whispered. "Time to act. And it looks like just the four of them."

"Right." Ronan pulled his seelion. "The men are soldiers, likely well-trained." He turned to the group, his face shadowed by the trees. "But they're also Iele, a dangerous breed. Watch your backs."

He nodded to Fiona's brother-in-law. "Jack, you and I take down the leading man. We take him out quick." Then he spoke to Sami and Tate. "You two use your magick on the other man while Fiona," he turned to her, "you go straight to Hellana. Make her understand why we're here."

"And I cover with my bow," Brit volunteered, already seeing how the strategy laid out.

Ronan gave a sharp nod. "Then let's do it. They're getting close." He pivoted around and flicked his fingers forward.

All at once, they surged in to attack.

The first soldier wielded a sword as a small cry went up from the older woman. But Hellana simply dropped to the ground when the second man released his hold and reached for his weapon as well.

He froze mid-motion, paralyzed by Tate and Sami's power, while Jack and Ronan made quick, bloody work of the one who'd drawn his blade.

The takedown of the warriors was dizzying in its speed, but Fiona had one directive, so it was to the ground she kneeled, speaking calmly to the new and much-abused mother. "Hellana. We're here to help you."

The Iele's blue eyes were dazed. "You … Who are … " In a blink her gaze cleared. "The Daughters of Nadia. The baby girls. You came to … help?"

"It's a long story," Fiona said, meeting her concerned gaze. "But we know what Emuirdane's planning. We want to save your baby, Hellana. Forget what's past. It's over and done."

Fiona gripped her shoulders, gently but firmly. "Just tell me where he took your son."

"The meeting point. Back up the trail," the white-haired woman interjected with confidence and clarity. She pointed up. "A third of the way, you'll see a side path. Follow it to the Circle of Syyrd. A large flat area rimmed by a circle of cairns."

"Stacks of rocks?" Fiona asked, checking that she'd understood.

"You can't miss it. The lead-away from the main pass is marked by a split tree."

Hellana grasped Fiona's arm. "Truly, you'll find my baby? You'll save him?"

"I swear to do everything in my power."

"He's gone to meet an evil Iele. King Malrik." Hellana gulped and ground through her teeth, "My father. You must be wary of him."

"We came ready to fight the Iele," Fiona said, glancing down at her dagger and being sure to keep it away from the two women.

"He is no simple Fae. You must heed me if you are to save my son."

With the distraught Hellana gripping her wrist, Fiona listened. And her blood turned cold.

25

"Someone needs to stay here with them." Fiona motioned to the two Iele women. Hellana was exhausted and emotionally drained, and her healer, Veloria, was well on in years. That they'd made it this far on foot was astounding, especially since Hellana had still been with child.

"Tate and I will stay," Jack offered, then studied the area. "Downriver, on the far side. We'll go through the water in case any hounds come back this way."

"And maybe I can conjure a scent." Tate shrugged. "A small spell to cover our tracks."

With the plan decided, Jack kneeled to Hellana, a woman he'd heard much about but had never met before tonight. Perhaps that was for the best.

He picked her up in his arms to carry her to the other riverbank where they would find a hiding place. Tate patted her dagger and pointed to Sami and Fiona. "Be careful up there, all of you. And be sure to come back."

"No worry there," Brit said. "You've got the key." He was referring to the polished white stone the Dea Matrona had given them, a one-way pass back to the mortal world. "Just don't lose it. I wouldn't want to spend eternity here." He gave Veloria a shamefaced smile. "No offense."

"None taken," she replied. "Just please find my lady's babe. Growing that child has changed her heart. I can't stand the thought of what it would do to her if—" She smothered the words and dissolved into tears.

"We'll find him," Fiona assured her before looking to the sky, where the two moons had almost merged into one. "But we have to go before it's too late."

"Yes, go. You have little time left." The old healer hurried after Tate, Jack, and Hellana.

Fiona walked to Sami who was standing over the two fallen Iele soldiers. "What about them?"

"This one's dead," Sami said dispassionately. "The injuries were shallow, but the gold did him in. The guy Tate and I subdued with magick is just sleeping it off."

"Sleeping what off?"

"The bump I gave him on his head." Sami quirked a brow as if expecting censure.

And looked surprised when Fiona said, "Good. I hope he stays out for a while. But let's drag him back behind the bushes anyway."

"Drag?" Palm facing outward, Sami pushed slightly through the air, and the unconscious man *whooshed* across the ground.

"Nice trick," Ronan said, then waved them to move. "Now let's cover some ground."

He didn't have to say what they were all thinking.

That they had to get up the hill and find the baby. Before they ran out of time.

Still mulling over what Hellana had told her, Fiona ran in silence, wondering how to phrase it for the others. She needed to tell them before they reached the Circle of Syyrd. But each time she practiced in her mind, horror shut her down, paralyzing her tongue and blocking the words.

She was still trying to work it out when a dark shape moved higher up on the pass. "Ronan," she said, coming to a stop, "I saw something. There." She pointed.

The others halted and drew their weapons. They strained to see what lurked beyond the curve.

A bloodcurdling howl carried through the dark.

Bloodhounds.

Someone gave a shrill whistle, and the beasts thundered down.

Fiona had forgotten how huge the things were, or how blood seeped from every single orifice. But her leg ached from the memory of their bites, and the tearing damage those jaws could deliver.

This time, however, the hounds were outnumbered.

And this time, she had her fire.

The first rip of flame stopped the lead dog, and it skidded to a halt in its big, bloody tracks.

Ronan sent his seelion flying, the blade slicing cleanly across its broad back. With one sharp whine, the huge beast dropped, before oozing across the ground in a thick red pool.

"The gold," Fiona said on a breath. "It only takes a nick."

A second hound bunched and lunged, heaving itself straight for her throat. And was struck midair by Brit's well-aimed bolt.

Another big mess, and another monster down. Then Sami used her magick on the last, sending her dagger straight to its heart.

Through the air, she retracted her blade. "Gross," she muttered with a grimace, wiping the hand that was now covered in muck.

Fiona started to smile at her sister, but her curving lips froze when a baby's cry echoed down from above.

"We've got to be close." Ronan sped off with Brit close behind, leaving Fiona and Sami to follow on their heels.

When they reached the split tree, they slowed their pace, moving with stealth until they knew what they'd find. Fiona edged up to Ronan, and together they peered around a large rock.

Emuirdane stood in the center of the circle, bordered on every side by pyramids of stacked, round stones. In his arms, he held the baby, small legs kicking with all his might.

Across from Emuirdane stood a bear of a man, his garments

plain and militaristic, shades of black from head to toe. "You're too late," he thundered out.

And for a split-second, Fiona feared he was talking to them.

"The Stag Moon is high. The deadline has passed." He spoke to Emuirdane with a sly curve of his lips.

"I am here now, and I have what you want." Emuirdane held out the child.

Fiona lurched, but Ronan put his arm out to catch her. "Wait," he whispered, his stare narrowed on the Iele who could only be King Malrik. Hellana's father.

And a different kind of monster.

Malrik stared with loathing at the bawling infant. "What is this? Where is the Ceffyl?"

"The Ceffyl is beyond our grasp. The mortal witches saw to that." Arms still extended, Emuirdane shook the child. "But you told me you would accept my blood. So take the brat and drink him dry!"

Sami sucked in a breath. "Drink him?" She curled her lip in revulsion. "What the hell is he talking about?"

"I should have told you before," Fiona said in a hush, "but things moved so fast. King Malrik is Hellana's father, and she told me that he is a different kind of Iele."

"One who drinks blood?" Brit shook his head, clearly as appalled as Sami. "What are they, some kind of . . . of . . ." Even he couldn't speak the name. The notion was simply too incredible.

"Vampyre." The word rushed from Ronan's lips, and his knuckles went white where he gripped his weapon. He shifted his eyes back to King Malrik. "Or something older. Something that came before."

Sami scowled. "But they still die from gold, right? And fire?"

Ronan turned away without reply.

It was Fiona who said, "Let's hope we don't have to find out."

Booming laughter rolled from the circle as the blood-sucking king thrust a hand toward the babe. "You think this whelp will satisfy me? That his blood will somehow pay your due?" More low laughter, though this time thick with derision. "I believe conceit has infected your mind, Emuirdane, to think I would forgive your debt for a pittance offer."

The laughter abruptly died. "Now. I want what is rightfully mine. You forfeited the contract." Malrik took a menacing stride toward Emuirdane. "And you know what that means."

"Here is the blood you seek!" Emuirdane's voice pitched higher. "My son who in his veins carries *my blood!*"

Only silence came from within the Circle of Syyrd. The tension in the air weighed on Fiona like a blanket of lead.

"This is your child?" Malrik asked. "Hellana's child?"

"Don't feign compassion for the infant, Malrik. You threw away your own daughter." Emuirdane had the gall to sound pompous. "You gave her to me, a man you *despise.*"

"I will not feed upon my kin."

"You care nothing for your kin! Now take him and drink!" Emuirdane seemed crazed, waving the baby to and fro. "Let us at last be done with this madness. Take the boy or nothing at all!"

Malrik raised his fists and roared like a beast, lunging for Emuirdane with hate in his eyes.

Too late, Emuirdane tried to run, but Malrik caught one arm and jerked him backward. The sudden shift in momentum lifted him off his feet.

And sent his small son sailing up through the air.

"No!" Fiona screamed, not caring that she'd revealed herself. She took a halting step forward just ahead of Ronan.

Dropping like a stone, the child fell toward the ground, its pitiful wail trailing through the night.

Ronan pushed himself forward and broke into a run.

Fiona just stopped, knowing she wouldn't make it. That neither of them would.

Only one thing could save Hellana's baby, so she channeled her magick and called upon it now.

Power exploded in her system and rushed to her hands, streaming from her palms like a river unleashed. Controlling the flow, she created a net. One she cast out swiftly, with a prayer on her lips.

And caught the small bundle just inches from the rocks.

The breath she expelled carried a sound of relief. Then she folded her arms as if cradling the child, and slowly reeled in the invisible strings. Hellana's baby—the child of her enemy—floated to her on a soft and gentle wave.

Locked in their own battle, the two kings struggled, grunting and cursing as they shoved, clawed, and bit. They paid no mind to Fiona and the others.

But Emuirdane's lone soldier charged with a shout.

Sword held high, the attacker swung down, but his blade glanced off of Ronan's uplifted seelion. The man bellowed in fury and raised his weapon again.

This time Ronan dropped his arm and angled his body, twisting his torso to carve his own blade across his opponent's abdomen. Instantly feeling the effects of gold, the Iele soldier collapsed and writhed in the dirt.

Fiona felt a tug on her elbow and spun to face Sami.

"We need to leave," her sister said, eyes wide with horror as she looked past Fiona to where Malrik had Emuirdane pinned.

Only then did Fiona hear the sounds. The obscene sound of guttural growls and snarls, the kind an animal made after a kill. When it was . . . *feeding*.

She didn't want to look. She couldn't stand to see. Holding the baby tighter, she quaked where she stood.

In an instant, Ronan was beside her, shoving her toward Sami and Brit. "Move. Move now," he said, his tone harsh with a sense of urgency, slicked over by repugnance and fear.

Seeing her own terror reflected in a soldier like Ronan was

enough to spur Fiona into action. But she'd barely taken a step when something smashed into a cairn near her feet. The stacked rocks tumbled and fell, demolished by what had flown through the air.

Fiona stared at the object, and her stomach heaved. She knew by the green stone, by the band of silver, that she was staring at Emuirdane's hand.

The growls behind her slowly morphed into words. "I'll take your blood, *and* your magick." She glanced back to see Malrik ripping into Emuirdane's neck, whose soulless black eyes had finally dimmed. They winked out entirely as his evil life drained into the soil.

"Here is the power!" Malrik reared up, his arms thrust over his head in triumph. And in his grasp, he held Emuirdane's brooch. "Here is my key!"

Fiona jerked her head back around and met Sami's wide eyes. Her sister had heard Malrik's cries, and now she too gazed down at the ring.

The murderous king's shouts echoed in Fiona's mind. And everything she'd ever known of Emuirdane's magick came flooding in. The power. The *key*.

She pictured the white stone, the Dea Matrona's token. "Could Emuirdane's stones work the same way?" she asked Sami, shaking her head in panicked denial.

"That's a chance we aren't going to take." In a flash, Sami grabbed Emuirdane's severed hand. She slipped off the ring and its malevolent green stone. "Let's go."

Brit stood several yards down the trail, his bow held high, covering their backs as they fled.

"Did he see us?" Fiona asked as they raced down the pass. "Did Malrik ever know we were there?" She'd been too concerned with rescuing the infant to be sure. But the king had been so engrossed with Emuirdane, so enthralled by the kill, she held out hope that he'd never noticed their presence.

"I can't be sure," Ronan said, his breath hitching as he ran beside her. "Here," he added when she almost tripped. "Let me take him."

For the sake of speed, she handed the baby to Ronan. And actually smiled to see how little the infant looked in his arms.

But now she moved much more quickly, and in minutes the four of them reached the base of the mountain and were soon splashing across a shallow stretch of the river. On the other side, Brit rasped out a call. "Tate. Jack."

"Over here." Tate stepped out from behind a huge tree and waved them over.

Walking now and able to catch their breaths, Ronan held out the baby. "You take him," he told Fiona. "You should be the one to give him back. I think this may mend many rifts," he said when she started to object.

"You're right." She nodded and accepted the bundle, and the baby who'd miraculously managed to fall asleep.

By the time they made it to the tree, Hellana was on her feet, her arms outstretched. "Oh, he's safe. He's alive and safe." She clutched her baby to her, then pulled back to inspect his sweet face. "You saved him for me."

Her ocean-blue eyes welled up as they fell upon Fiona. "Why? Why would you help me? When I would have slaughtered you in your own crib?"

"Because he has nothing to do with hate or vengeance. He is an innocent." Fiona met Hellana's eyes and spoke with sincerity. "And he has a chance to grow up loved, to be a better person than his father."

"Or his mother," Hellana whispered, and simply broke down in tears. "How can I ever make amends for the past? I know a mother's love now, and yours must surely despise me for all I've done."

"Our mother is a forgiving sort," Sami said stepping closer. She opened her mouth, and Fiona swore she would add, "But I'm not."

Instead, Sami took a closer took at the infant and her expression simply melted. "Just don't make us regret this, Hellana. Emuirdane is dead now, so—"

Hellana gasped.

"You can take this opportunity to make a difference with your son," Sami continued, tickling the baby's chin.

"Aye, listen to them, my dove." The old woman emerged from the shadows. "Raise the boy well, for he will one day be king." She wrapped an arm around Hellana's shoulders, and in the gesture, in her eyes, Fiona saw the shine of love.

"Yes." Hellana put her head to the woman's. Then she jerked up. "And I am now the ruling queen. Emuirdane is gone, and I govern in his stead."

"So when that fool of a guard wakes, he'll answer to *you*." Veloria wagged a finger. "We should rouse him and get the two of you back to the castle. You need your rest."

"Before you do that." Sami slid her hand into her pocket, then retrieved Emuirdane's ring. "We came away with this," she said and paused, "because of your father. He went a little crazy up there. He took Emuirdane's brooch that held the similar green stone. He raved about power and—"

"My father has the brooch?" Hellana's face drained of what little color it had.

"Yes," Fiona answered.

"Then you must take the ring out of this world. Take it away where he can never find it." Hellana ran a hand through her sea-blue hair. "Together the stones provide too much magick."

Sami shoved it back in her pocket. "Copy that."

"Now. We need to get the babe home," the older woman said to Hellana, guiding her toward the river.

Hellana stopped and turned back, staring at each of the sisters. "Thank you for what you've done. I can never repay you, but if you ever find yourselves in need," she bowed her head, "I am in your debt."

As the two women strolled over the grass with the tiny king to be, Tate held out the white stone, the key the goddess had given them so they could transport home. "Let's use this now and get out of this gloomy realm."

"I'm all for that," Brit said, as he, Jack, and Ronan crowded in close.

Standing in a circle, the six of them focused on the stone. And just as they'd been instructed, they pictured the place they wanted to go.

In a quick and dazzling burst of white, they were back home in the kitchen.

Fiona's mother and grandfather sat at the table, both brooding into cups of tea. And both jumped to their feet with cries of joy.

"You're back, all of you!" Granddad called out as Fiona's mother rushed to embrace them one by one.

Fiona laughed and accepted her hug, then met Ronan's smiling eyes when he got one too.

Then Nadia drew back with a clap of her hands. "Right. I'm cooking." She went to the pantry. "And while I do, I want to hear everything."

Sami and Brit launched into the story of the baby, and how Emuirdane had met his bloody end, while Tate and Jack sat back down with Granddad, assuring him they were all just fine.

With her family occupied, Fiona pulled Ronan over to the large bay window. Night had fallen in this world as well, and a single white moon looked peacefully down.

"Ronan," she whispered, touching his face. "I know you have to go, back to Faerie to fulfill your duty."

"I do," he said, pulling her in with a heartfelt sigh, lowering his forehead to hers in his endearing way.

"I was hoping, though, you could stay one more night." She

nuzzled his neck as his arms stole around her waist. "Just one more."

She felt his kiss on the top of her head. "The Legion in its entirety couldn't drag me away." He lifted her chin so she could meet his eyes. "Not before you love me again."

Her heart swelled as her eyes welled up. "I'll love you enough to last forever."

"You won't have to wait forever, my sweet, green-eyed witch."

"Promise me?" Her voice caught on a sob. "Swear you'll come back."

"To you, Fiona? I will always come back." And the moon shone brighter, a cool wash of white, when their lips met and hearts collided.

And they sealed the promise with a kiss.

Suza Kates writes both paranormal romance and romantic suspense. She lives in Savannah, Georgia with her family and four ridiculously spoiled cats.

For more on Suza and her books visit

www.suzakates.com